# RAISED ON ROCK

David Owen Ferrier

Battle Press

SATELLITE BEACH, FLORIDA

RAISED ON ROCK

Copyright © 2023 by David Ferrier.

All rights reserved. No part of this book may be used or reproduced by any means, graphic, electronic or mechanical, including photocopying, recording, taping or by any information storage retrieval system without the written permission of the author or publisher except in the case of brief quotations embodied in critical articles and reviews.

Battle Press books may be ordered through booksellers or by contacting:

Battle Press
1588 Highway A1A #B
Satellite Beach, FL 32937
1-919-218-4039
steve@battlepress.media
www.battlepress.media

ISBN: 979-8-9873-3795-0 (softcover)

ISBN: 979-8-9873-3796-7 (eBook)

Library of Congress Control Number: 2023901212

First Edition.

Sing in me Muse,
of Later Days,

When Children
Spoke Their Own
Words
And Made Their
Own Music.

# Dedication:

**To My Wife, Debi, Who Saves Me
From me.**

**To The Patient Encouragers.**

**You know who you are.**

**AND TO THE SNORTER, A
GREAT, GREAT DOGGIE.**

# Prologue

The teen years were, for me, the uncertain years. Puberty, insecurity, conformity and rebellion all combined to create, and destroy me. I wasn't a kid anymore, yet certainly not a grown up either. Teenaged, "just in-between aged", were the years of confusion, confidence, heartache and harmony.

I, along with my friends, fell in love, lust, despair and delight, sometimes all in the same day. And all of this "Ball of Confusion" was powered by the pounding, pulsating, penetrating rhythms of Top 40, AM Radio, Rock & Roll Music, (Any old way you choose it).

These melodies became our heartbeats, our goodness and our badness, our poetry and our philosophy. From it we received advice, wisdom and glee, while all the time our toes were tapping and the beat was in our feet.

There are twenty stories here. The continuing adventures, if you will, of David and Teddy and Margaret Mary along with all of their friends and family in the years between 1964 and 1967.

I hope you will remember, as I have come to do, that we were all growing older, if not up.

# MUSIC

It has the power to make us smile,
And bring us to all kinds of tears.
It can carry us back in time,
And inspire us to dance in the moment.
For all our happiest days,
There is music.

## ROCK & ROLL

"It's reckless and rude. It's defiant and daring. It's a fist shaken at age. It's a voice that screams out questions because the answers keep changing. The very young play it because they are searching for some way to express their anger and joy, their confusion and dreams."

-Nora Roberts

# Table Of Contents

# THE BEATLES

## I SAW HER STANDING THERE
## I WANT TO HOLD YOUR HAND

# Chapter One

## *I Want To Hold Your Hand Forever*

"Paul is the cutest! I think he's dreamy!"

"I like George, he's the shy one with wonderful eyes."

This is Margaret Mary talking. My Margaret Mary. About George Harrison, one of The Beatles! She's talking with Linda Rogers, the one who thinks Paul is the cutest. Paul McCartney, another Beatle!

I couldn't believe it. You wouldn't know about Margaret Mary unless you read a book called **"Born On A Mountaintop,"** which is all about me and her and my friends when we were little kids. We are grown up now, Teenagers, in High School, Young Adults, practically. This is why I can hardly believe what I'm hearing. You see, Margaret Mary is my North Star, my go-to person for common sense and good judgment, the most sensible and level headed of my childhood companions. And now she has gone goofy over four long haired guys from England who sang some songs on the Ed Sullivan show last Sunday night, February 9, 1964.

Margaret Mary came over to my house to watch the show because she doesn't have a TV at her house. Her father, Sean Patrick, says they are a nuisance, a "distraction to the higher contemplations." Margaret Mary agreed with her father, mostly. Teddy, he's my other best friend, came too.

He's got a TV but we all wanted to watch the show together because The Beatles! were all anyone at school had talked about all week. Even before they were going to be on TV, The Beatles! were everywhere. Their songs got played on WMEX and WBZ, our favorite radio stations, over and over. They weren't only IN the top ten records, they WERE the top ten records! "I Want To Hold Your Hand", "She Loves You", "Please, Please Me", "Love Me Do", "I Saw Her Standing There", "P.S. I Love You", played relentlessly over the radio and in our heads. The morning news, news at noon, the evening news, broadcasted every move these guys made, every wave from a hotel window or frantic rush to a waiting limousine. They were calling it "Beatlemania" and I guess that's what it was, whatever that meant.

As Beatle Mania continued to overwhelm the airwaves, a full scale "British Invasion" of bizarre, long-haired, Cockney sounding rock & rollers started changing forever the sounds in our heads. There were the Rolling Stones, kind of Bad Boy Beatles, the Dave Clark Five, kind of shouting Beatles, the Searchers, the Hollies, Gerry and the Pacemakers, the Zombies, the Animals and lots of really cool, skinny English chicks in very short plastic dresses. Suddenly Rock and Roll came alive again, like the pound of our pulses and the beats of our heart once school was out and the jukeboxes called our names.

"Did you like them David?" Margaret Mary asked, drawing me into the conversation as she could see I was going into my recently well-rehearsed adolescent sulk.

"Yeah," I grunted. "They were okay, I guess."

"They looked real weird with that long hair and everything," Teddy added, cutting to the quick, as he always did.

"Well, I think they're fabulous," Linda replied with Margaret Mary nodding in agreement.

"Are you going to grow a Beatle haircut, David?" Linda kidded, I hoped.

"David is more of an Elvis guy," Margaret Mary said, squeezing my arm affectionately.

Actually I hadn't been much of an "Elvis guy" since I saw him playing a ukulele and singing to puppets in the movies. Lately Rock & Roll had degenerated to songs about Purple People Eaters, Itsy Bitsy Teenie Weenie, Yellow Polka Dot Bikinis, Hound Dog, Men and the Duke of Earl. Chuck Berry was in jail, Little Richard found Jesus and lost his piano, somebody shot Sam Cooke and the Everly Brothers were in the Marine Corps. Rock & Roll was a mess, until The Beatles! came along, and everything changed.

Despite our freshly found enjoyment of The Beatles! the world continued to spin, in some cases, not so well. Nightly newscasts veered from the aftermath of President Kennedy's murder to strange reassurances that we would not be sending American boys off to fight in an Asian war very few of us even knew was happening. New president Lyndon Johnson muttered these reassurances while he was having his picture taken along with generals and admirals who were grinning like wolves. And in a far away place called Saigon, strange Asian men in Orange robes were setting themselves on fire in the streets.

Peter Rayburn, black beret and all, was home from his prep school on vacation and was all over this. "Wait and see," he predicted, "there's a lot more going to come out about all this stuff."

Teddy too, thought he smelled a crook, somewhere.

But there were no crooks, no looming conflicts in our heads that crisp, snowy winter morning as we crunched our way along the wintry sidewalks toward Lowell High school.

"I'm buying their record right after school today. I can't wait!" Linda Rogers proclaimed.

"They are going to be on TV again next week," Margaret Mary added, with a little more enthusiasm than I would have liked.

"Yeah, and the week after that too," Teddy said, "My sister, Connie read it in the TV Guide."

I began to realize these guys weren't going away for a while, dreamy eyes and all.

The other issue that wasn't going away lingered in the shadows of Margaret Mary's home as she clung hopelessly to her shattered father, Sean Patrick, now deeply lost in the whiskey. His reaction to the gunfire in Dallas last fall was days and weeks of insensate drinking before he was placed on a merciful sabbatical by the college. He would not be saved, not by Keats, not by Browning, not by his devoted, terrified daughter. He spent his days shuffling about the house in tattered robe and slippers, dressing only to shamble to the liquor store to buy more whiskey. Margaret Mary begged, pleaded and prayed for his recovery, though the miracle would not appear. She began to miss days of school, then entire weeks, afraid to leave her father's side. I carried schoolwork to her, brought her books, found her flowers, offered her favorite minted candy, but could not ease the anxiety that enveloped her.

Finally, a drunken stumble on a winter night opened a gaping, bloody gash on Sean Patrick's forehead sending an ambulance screaming from their home in the middle of the night. Margaret Mary and I followed behind with my father at the wheel of our family car, racing to Saint Joseph's hospital where the medicine was stored.

Once stitches were stitched and bandages turbaned, Sean Patrick caught sight of his devastated daughter, collapsed in a chair at the foot of his hospital bed. Mercifully the candle within him flickered, then glowed once again from his deep, personal darkness and he could see once again beyond his misery.

That became Sean's last drunken evening, or day. He went from the medical ward to the alcohol treatment ward and for ten excruciating days, dried out. He emerged, not his old self, but a new self, hesitant in his thoughts and speech, wary of the world around him, frail and dependent, leaning heavily into Margaret Mary, draining her of her childhood, robbing me of the girl I had come to realize I loved.

We remained close, as friends, as she became full time caretaker to her father's frailty. There were no more record hops, fast or slow dances, or holding of hands as we walked along. There was only an awakened, ongoing dread in Margaret Mary, a terror she finally shared one night as we sat together on her front porch.

"What if he dies?" She whispered to me as Sean lay sleeping within the house. "The doctor said if he starts drinking again it will kill him, and he always starts drinking again."

"Maybe he won't," I offered. "He promised he wouldn't."

"He's promised before, I can't even tell you how many times."

And then she buried her face in my shoulder and sobbed. I felt helpless, aching to think of something I could say or do to ease her pain, ashamed of my helplessness.

"All of his family is back in Ireland. I don't even know them." Margaret Mary sat up straight and continued, "My mother's parents are both dead. She has a sister back in Ohio, we get a Christmas card from her every year but I don't know her. There is no one else."

"There's me," I finally managed to say. "No matter what happens, there's me." It was as much a prayer as a promise.

"I know that," she sighed, leaning once again into my shoulder. "But where would I live? How could I support myself?" Her voice was fragile, frail, frightened.

The silence which filled the room had gotten very loud when I swallowed hard and said, "Maybe we could get married or something."

Margaret Mary sat straight up and looked at me, hard. Then her eyes softened and she replied, "Oh David, we're only fifteen years old. That wouldn't help the problem, it would only make it twice as big."

As she leaned forward and kissed my cheek we heard a soft rustling of footsteps from within the darkened house. Sean

Patrick, lost in sad, plaid pajamas and shabby robe and slippers stood in the doorway. He looked old and frail. He was crying. In his hands he held a large brown envelope, thick with papers.

"My children," he began, wiping away his tears as he joined us on the porch. "I heard what you were saying and it is breaking my heart."

Sean took a chair across from us. Pressing his hands together as if in prayer he continued, "And now I would like to speak to you about these things that frighten you."

"I can leave if you want," I said, starting to rise from the sofa, Margaret Mary tugged me back down beside her. She said nothing but it was pretty clear she wanted me to stay. I stayed.

Sean emptied the thick brown envelope onto the floor in front of him. Picking up scraps of paper he spoke of insurance policies and savings accounts, endowments and inheritances, mortgages and assets, all the accoutrements of fiscal life. All directed at, and for the benefit of Margaret Mary.

She took all this in, in her very grown up fashion, me sitting silent beside her. When Sean finished she stood up and crossed the room, putting her arms around him.

"Daddy, I don't need any of those things, I just need you," She said, sounding just like a little girl.

They were quiet together, father and daughter comforting one another. Then Sean straightened in his chair and spoke in a low soft voice, "I know I am broken with the whiskey. It is a crutch I sometimes find I cannot walk without. But I promise you now, as I have too many times before, but I promise you anyway, I have put that crutch aside. I would rather limp, rather not walk at all, than hurt you."

In the silence that followed I stood up to leave. Margaret Mary did not try to stop me. As I opened the porch door Margaret Mary came to me and walked with me outside. We stopped on the sidewalk in front of her house and she said, "Thank you for being my very special, best friend." Her eyes were filled with tears. I nodded, choked up myself, and hugged her goodnight.

As I turned to walk home she called after me, "And thank you for asking me to marry you."

Linda Rogers bought "Introducing The Beatles, England's No. 1 Vocal Group," at Record Lane right after school that Monday. For an entire week she and Margaret Mary played it over and over, swooning to the tunes.

Eventually Sean returned to teaching. Margaret Mary hummed Beatle tunes and smiled again. I scowled less and began to think maybe I would let my hair get a little longer.

*Listen, Do you want to know a secret?*
*Do you promise not to tell?*
*Closer, let me whisper in your ear,*
*Tell you words you long to hear.*
*I'm in love with you.*

And, of course, I was.

"The music of your youth stays with you throughout your life." **-Dick Clark** American Bandstand

<u>"Do You Want To Know A Secret"</u>, Lennon/McCartney (mostly Lennon), released March 3, 1963. The first Beatles top ten single, #2 on Billboard Charts to feature George Harrison as lead singer.

"Nothing lifts my spirits more than driving around in my car listening to very loud Rock N Roll music."

-Debi F.

# Chapter Two

## *Drive My Car*

"Easy, easy on the gas pedal. Don't stomp on it."

This is my Dad, speaking patiently, calmly as I jerked and staggered the family station wagon around the frozen parking lot of Cawley Memorial Stadium in the frigid New England winter of 1964.

I turned sixteen on my last birthday and sixteen meant to me, and all my friends, one thing above all else; Learner's Permit, the teen age prelude to a driver's license. My Ticket to Ride.

"That's it. Slow down a little, keep it straight."

I had mastered, sort of, driving in a straight line, in a large, open parking lot with my Dad right next to me. Not right next to me, he stayed over on the passenger side, showing confidence that I wouldn't spin out of control and wreck the car. My Dad was like that, letting me know that he trusted me to do the right thing. The worst feeling in the world for me is when I felt like I let my Dad down. I seriously tried to keep that sort of thing to a minimum.

"Now press on the brake, slow. That's it. Keep your foot on the brake, come to a full stop and put the car in Park."

I slid the lever into the right position and relaxed my foot on the brake.

"How'd I do, Dad?"

"You did just fine, all it takes is practice."

This wasn't the first time my Dad had let me drive. We had come last week but the parking lot was too icy. I spent as much time going sideward as I did forward. My Dad suggested we try it on another day. This other day.

"My turn now Mr. Ferrier? My turn?" Teddy chirped from the back seat. He was hopping with excitement, much more than ready to get behind the wheel.

"Okay, you and Dave trade places."

And we did. Two more times that frosty Saturday morning while my Dad showed us how to turn left, and right, speed up, slow down, even back up, which was going to take more practice. When we were finished neither Teddy nor I could stop grinning.  We coulda' killed us a bear.

"You both did real good," my Dad said, "but this is a parking lot. Driving gets a lot more complicated out there on the streets. How about we call it a day and go find a jelly donut?"

Days didn't get much better than this.

In the past few months Teddy and I had gradually outgrown our bicycles, baseball cards, comic books and other "kid stuff". Walt Disney no longer enchanted us. "The Twilight Zone" and "Combat!" had replaced Spin and Marty and Bugs Bunny, even Davy Crockett. Playboy magazine peeked out from our secret hiding places while Superman and Batman receded from relevance. Choices about grown up things which were once way down a far off road were now scary stuff, immediate concerns. College board exams, draft cards, military service, high school graduation were now right under our noses.

Personal heartbreaks, like Margaret Mary's ongoing struggles with Sean Patrick had been leavened somewhat by "The Beatles!", the World Champion Boston Celtics, an exciting film about the battle of Roarke's Drift called "ZULU!" and a forbidden, dog-eared paperback book secretly passed around called "The Carpetbaggers".

Matt Dillon still kept Dodge City safe, though I was becoming more interested in Miss Kitty at the Long Branch. Ben Cartwright still ran the Ponderosa with three never leaving home bachelor sons and Wagon Train continued to roll along without ever arriving anywhere. Cowboys and bad guys were everywhere on our TV sets. Clean cut heroes and easily identified and vanquished villains were the recipe of the TV screen, though real life was becoming more murky each day.

Yet all that was pushed aside as we slid into the plastic booth at Paradise Donuts after our driving lesson. Teddy and I had still not stopped smiling as my Dad ordered hot chocolates, coffee and delicious fresh donuts.

When my Dad brought the tray of goodies to the table and slid in across from us, Teddy immediately asked, "Who taught you to drive, Mr. Ferrier?"

My Dad took a sip of his coffee and put down his plain donut, he called them sinkers, and answered, "I learned in the Army, down at Fort Hood, Texas. I never drove a car before I went into the Army."

"Really, Dad? How come?" Another thing I never knew about my Dad.

"We never had a family car while I was growing up, most families didn't. Your grandfather didn't make a lot of money in those days. If we needed to go somewhere we walked or took the bus."

"Did'ja ever get to drive a tank?" Teddy spoke out from under his powdered sugar mustache, eager to know.

My Dad laughed, "No tanks, Teddy. A jeep or two, small trucks, I did more marching than driving."

My Dad hardly ever talked about his Army days. I knew he was a tail gunner, in B-24 bombers during World War II. There were some pictures and memorabilia in a big old box down in the basement of our Glenmere Street home. I hoped he would talk a little more about them. Instead he changed the subject.

"Teddy, I'm going to sign Dave up for driving school. You should talk to your Dad about going too. It makes the car insurance a lot cheaper."

We had already talked about this at home. Driving school costs forty dollars. I was going to pay half out of my Lefty's pay, my Dad would pay the rest. It felt real good to be paying my share. Kind of grown up.

"My father already said it was okay," Teddy replied, "On account of he's too busy to teach me himself."

Teddy's father was always too busy. My Dad hardly ever was. He had taught me how to ride a bike, catch ground balls, tie a tie, comb my hair and swim in the ocean. He always made time for me and for my brothers who got all the same lessons I did. We learned to play cribbage on rainy nights in York Beach, Maine, catch flounder on foggy Saturday mornings in York Harbor, catch, throw and kick baseballs and footballs in our Big Oak backyard on Glenmere Street, and pray as a family every Sunday morning at the Immaculate Conception church. Some of these lessons would wear off over the years, others would be with me all my life.

"Did you like being in the Army Dad?" I was trying to get the conversation back on track. My track.

"Most of the time. I missed your mother a lot and my family, but I needed to be where I was, doing what I was doing."

"Dave says you were dropping bombs on those Nazi guys," Teddy said.

"Well, I wasn't dropping the bombs, I was in the back of the plane hoping nobody would drop a bomb on me."

My Dad smiled and finished his sinker, took a last gulp of his coffee and brushed off his hands.

"C'mon you two, David, you have to be at work and I told your father I would drop you off at the garage on the way by Teddy."

Teddy was working with his father at the garage on weekends when he wasn't training down at Nelson's Gym.

I realized my Dad did not like to talk a lot about his Army days and I wondered why. I hoped someday we could talk about it, but for now, this Saturday morning, the discussion was over. Work beckoned me and Teddy, a prelude to all the grown up business just ahead.

As much as I wanted to get my driver's license, I still felt a pang when I walked by my forsaken blue bike leaning in the corner of the garden shed. Every now and then I rifled through my baseball cards, yesterday's treasures languishing in a shoe box that would disappear over the years. Kid stuff for sure but that part of me hadn't faded quite yet, though I kept this a carefully guarded secret.

In due time there was a driving test at the Registry of Motor Vehicles, a supervised cruise through Lowell's back streets with Mr. Lankin, of the Wannalancit Driving School of which Teddy and I were both graduates. With a wink and a nod Mr. Lankin introduced us to the Registry guy, who had an ominous clipboard and needed a shave. First me, then Teddy maneuvered through the back streets of Lowell, stopping on a hill, backing up, turning left and right and finally parking in the Registry parking lot. The Registry Guy got out, told us he'd be right back after he figured up our scores and we waited, the longest twenty minutes of my life so far, until he reemerged from the building, looking grim and official. Neither Teddy nor I spoke as he gave another secret nod and smile to Mr. Lankin and then handed us each our pink slip, our Learner's Permit, the Ticket To Ride.

There we were, Teddy and I once again, grinning so wide we coulda' kilt us another bear, and feeling as proud as I ever had in my life. I couldn't wait to show Margaret Mary, to show my Mom and Dad and to go for a ride in the family car all by myself.

Mr. Lankin dropped Teddy and me off at Shedd Park. We still hadn't stopped grinning but there was nobody around to show our prizes to. We walked home together talking about car rides and road trips, near destinations and far. Teddy went home to tell Connie and his father. I strutted into our living room proud as punch. My Mom gave me a big hug, my brothers both wanted to see my new license and as we all celebrated my Dad came home. He knew without asking what had happened and smiled as proudly as I felt. Then he tossed me the keys to the car, his car, the family car and said,

"Why don't you take us all out for a drive? Nichols ice cream maybe? This calls for a celebration."

Days didn't get any better than this. And Chuck Berry told us so.

*Ridin' along in my automobile.*

*My baby beside me at the wheel,*

*I stole a kiss at the turn of a mile,*

*My curiosity running wild.*

*Cruisin and playin' the radio,*

*With no particular place to go.*

"No Particular Place To Go", Chuck Berry, released May 1964. Reached #10 on Billboard charts. Berry was a master of the "car" song, a master of "R&R Music". John Lennon was quoted as saying, "If you had to give Rock&Roll another name, you might call it Chuck Berry."

# What A Boxer Knows

1. Hard work makes champions. They are not born that way.

2. Sacrifice and success go together like trust and brotherhood.

3. You don't lose when you get knocked down. You lose when you stay down.

4. When you control your emotions you control the fight.

5. Toughness starts in the mind.

6. The main ingredient in victory is sweat.

7. Respect your opponent or he won't respect you.

8. If you can't trust the people in your corner, get another corner.

9. Winning isn't everything. Doing your best is.

10. Believe in yourself. You are all you have in the ring.

-Max Ginsburg

# Chapter Three

## *Screwloose*

The concrete floor in Nelson's Gym still frosted my toes, channeling the not yet springtime cold through my sneakers and socks and making the hair on my legs stand stiff as a wire brush. You had to keep moving to stay warm at Nelson's Gym and that's what I was doing this March morning a month or so after the Beatles had "yeah, yeah, yeah'd" their way into our lives. I had driven myself to the gym, parking proudly outside, hoping everybody inside would notice.

Teddy was inside, skipping rope in a corner. Paco Barnes was laughing with The Prince and Antoine while Screwloose lurked around the speed bags making machine gun noises with his fists.

"Look here, a ghost!" Antoine announced with his "ksk, ksk, ksk" of a laugh as I walked over. Teddy dropped his jump rope and joined us with a big smile.

"Thought you had to work today?" He seemed surprised and pleased.

"Lefty gave me the day off. He's starting a new kid, his nephew or something," I replied.

"Neffhew, huh," Screwloose grunted though I wasn't aware he was listening.

I returned to the gym to get some exercise, break a sweat, and lighten the late winter gloom of Lowell, Massachusetts. I needed a distraction, something I could do well, boxing was all that.

During the Christmas school break I had eaten several lunches with Peter Rayburn, still on fire with the rapidly emerging notion that Lee Harvey Oswald had not acted alone and that much more than we were being told was afoot regarding the death of our President in Dallas.

 Only last week, Jack Ruby, who had shockingly killed Oswald in the basement of the Dallas Police Department three days after the president was killed, was found guilty of murder and sentenced to death after a hushed and hasty trial where he was defended pro bono by noted defense attorney Melvin Belli. Ruby, a Dallas based, mobbed up gangster sat mute at his trial, offering only that he wanted to save Jackie Kennedy the pain of an Oswald murder trial as his motivation for the killing. Mobbed up gangsters, who run strip clubs are like that, really nice guys. Or so we were told.

Peter Rayburn wasn't buying this and neither were a growing number of journalists and emerging "conspiracy theorists". A reporter named Mark Lane had come right out and said Oswald was the "patsy" he claimed to be right after his arrest. In a magazine article that Peter Rayburn carried with him like a flag, Mark Lane sowed major seeds of doubt surrounding President Kennedy's death, reopening the wound, prolonging the sorrow.

Even Margaret Mary seemed skeptical that a crime of such magnitude could have been perpetrated by a dopey little guy like Lee Harvey Oswald. Her father, Sean Patrick, could only murmur, "Murder will out, my children," as he tightened his grip on sobriety.

Such was the bile that was welling up within me during these bleak times. School had become a slog, as gray and lifeless as our winter city. "The Beatles!" were still Beatling and Margaret Mary had come back to life, although not so much in my life. As we trundled toward the end of our junior year in high school Margaret Mary had become fixated on college and college board examinations, the "where and when and how" of life after high school. She would ask me my plans as she speculated on her own. College was for her an oncoming certainty. For now, I preferred boxing.

Only two weeks earlier Cassius Clay, a brash 7-1 underdog, had shocked the world by defeating Sonny Liston for the heavyweight championship of the world. Shocked the world perhaps, but not Teddy, who guaranteed a Clay victory.

"That guy Liston looks like a crook to me," Teddy proclaimed. Pretty soon we were going to have to start listening more carefully to Teddy.

"You wanna' hit the bag?" Teddy offered.

"You best be careful that bag don't be hittin' you. You ain't been around in a while." The Prince had a point.

"Maybe I'll use the rope for a while," I answered. "Loosen up."

Besides my legs were freezing. Teddy tossed me his jump rope and I repaired to a corner to skip and hop and warm myself up.

Once I got into the rhythm I was fine, feeling good as the activity in the gym swirled around me. I was a little envious of how easily Teddy interacted with everyone. He had been spending a lot of time there, making friends inside and outside the gym. Me, I was more of a tourist, splitting my time between schoolwork, my job at Lefty's, my relationship with Margaret Mary, and prime time TV.

But for now, right now, this Saturday morning, I was bouncing around, getting back into fighting shape and shaking off my winter ills.

When my legs tired of the rope I moved over to the heavy bag and began lightly tapping away, getting my rhythm back, enjoying the burn in my arms and the solid smacks of my gloves on the canvas bag. After a rapid series of left-right-lefts, and a little ducking and weaving, I stepped back, out of breath and satisfied. I blew out some frosty air and bounced on my toes a bit until Screwloose ambled over. He did not look at me when he asked, "You think maybe that Lefty guy be givin' me a job, like washin' dishes or sumthin'?"

I stopped bouncing and considered the wiry, black fighter I knew only as a shadow in the gym, one I only knew by the name of Screwloose. This was the longest conversation we ever had and it was only one question long.

I had been told, several times, that Screwloose was, well, volatile. He was certainly a mystery to me, as well as the rest of the guys at the gym. He was there every time I came, training apart, but around the rest of the group. This was our first talk and I was unsure of how to reply.

"I, uh, don't know," I began, "I could ask Lefty for you but we don't use dishes, it's all paper plates and wax cups."

"Still maybe he need someone to clean up," He answered.

"For that he's got nephews," I said, "and me."

"Just askin' is all, I needs to make me some money."

"Uh," I began, and this was embarrassing, "I don't know your real name, I'd have to know that, you know, to ask Lefty."

"Lester," he replied. "My real name be Lester. I'm named after my uncle Lester. He my mother's brother. He in the Navy, or he was. He drownded."

"Lester what?" I asked. "Lefty would want to know your whole name." I don't know why but I was sort of apologizing for asking this.

"Lester Judge, my Daddy's name be Arthur Judge when he was married to my Mama."

Lester and I moved over to a bench by the wall and we sat down. I saw Teddy, Antoine and the others watching us out of the corner of their eyes.

"Where's your father now? You said, 'when he was your father.'" The more I spoke with Lester the more I wanted to know about him.

"He still my father, but he live in Minny-apple-less. That's out near Chicago somewhere I think."

"Are they divorced, your mother and father?" I didn't know how far I could go with my questions but Screwloose, now Lester, didn't seem to mind.

"Don't know. But he don't live with us no more. He live in Minny-apple-less because he thinks my Momma's crazy. Said he can't live with her no more but that when I turn eighteen I can come live with him. I be turnin' eighteen next month, that's why I needs me some money."

"So you can go live with your father?" I asked. Screwloose nodded, still not looking at me. This was a lot of information. I was really interested to hear more.

"Can I ask you a question?" I began cautiously.

"That's all you been doin'," He replied. "It's all right though."

"Why do," I hesitated not sure how to walk this ground, "Do you mind that people call you Screwloose?"

"Screwloose my street name. People got to call me sumptin."

"They could call you Lester."

"Don't like Lester. My uncle was a fool."

I was getting in over my head here.

"Lookit," he continued, "callin' somebody Screwloose that ain't such a bad thing, you know? Everybody got a screw loose somewhere is what I think. Ain't nobody perfect."

I had no answer for that, so I asked another question. "Do you have any brothers or sisters?"

"Just me and my Momma. She crazy, like my Daddy says, talks out loud to Jesus all the time. Says he talk back to her too. Like I said, screwloose."

"Would you mind if I called you Lester?"

"Don't need to have you callin' me nuthin', lest you telling me that Lefty guy gonna' hire me to wash dishes."

Screwloose stood up, shook his head from side to side, started to bounce on his feet, loosening up.

"You know why my Uncle Lester drownded? Couldn't swim. Why would a man, couldn't swim, join the Navy? Screwloose, just like everybody else."

And Screwloose, no longer Lester, wandered back into the gym.

I sat on the bench a while longer, thinking. After a while I got up and went back over to the heavy bag. Hitting it felt better than thinking about Screwloose's chance of getting hired at Lefty's, but I was going to ask anyway.

Which I did, two days later. Lefty said no. He had a lot of nephews. I was back in the gym that weekend and Screwloose was there, lurking on the edges, as usual. What was not usual was I went right over to him after I changed and taped up.

"I talked to Lefty. He said he doesn't need any more help right now."

"Got them neff-hews huh?" He snorted. "I 'preciate you askin' for me though."

At that point Screwloose went his way and I mine. I banged the heavy bag for a while then moved onto the practice mat for some shadow boxing. As the weeks passed I was getting into pretty good shape. One morning I went three thumping rounds with Paco Barnes who was getting ready to fight in the Golden Gloves. Butchie, now Kevin, was training for the Golden Gloves as well and looked good in the ring. I didn't spar with Butchie. When he faced off with The Prince everybody in the gym gathered around to watch. Teddy was going to fight this year as well. He had stuck to his training a lot more than I had and was miles ahead of me as a boxer. We sparred together a time or two but it didn't work out. I didn't want to hit him and he didn't want to hit me.  We were still buddies.

Then on a Saturday morning two weeks after I talked to Lefty, Paco Barnes exploded into the gym with the news.

"You guys hear what happened to Screwloose!" He shouted as he burst through the doors. Max peeked out of his office then joined the crowd that was gathering around Paco.

"He got killed last night. The cops shot him. He was with some guys robbing a liquor store!" Paco exclaimed.

"Shot him in the back and he didn't even have a gun!" Antoine, who had followed Paco into the gym added.

There was an angry growl in the room, bad air filled the space. Paco continued, "Finnegan's Liquor, out on the boulevard. Him and two other guys."

"Where'd you hear about this?" Max asked.

"I was getting my paycheck down at the Sun just now. It's gonna' be in tonight's paper." Antoine drove a delivery truck for the Lowell Sun.

"How 'bout you Paco? Where'd you hear it?" Max asked.

"My cousin seen it. He was out on the boulevard last night and seen all the cop cars. He went over there and saw what happened."

"He saw the cops shoot Screwloose?" Butchie asked.

"Nah, but he seen the car and the blood and everything," Paco replied.

Anger, hurt, confusion filled the gym. I was feeling very sad for the guy who needed some money to go see his father in Minny-Apple-Less.

"I'm gonna' make a call or two, see what I can find out," Max said and headed for his office. The rest of us clustered around Paco and Antoine sharing shock, indignation and memories of the guy most of us knew only as Screwloose. After several minutes Max came out of his office and asked us to gather around.

"I called Jimmy Gannon down at the Sun. Told him Lester was one of our fighters and could he find out what had happened. Jimmy's comin' over. You guys need to hear what went on last night."

Jimmy Gannon was a sports writer down at the Sun. He covered boxing and knew Max and most of us pretty well. With that we waited, one eye on the door as we bounced around to stay warm. About forty minutes later Jimmy Gannon arrived with two police officers, a Captain we didn't know and Billy Toussiant, a guy who used to train at the gym before he joined the police department. Several of the fighters looked at the police officers with open hostility. Max came out of his office and we gathered around to hear what they had to say.

Jimmy started. "I know you guys have heard about Lester. There's a rumor going around that he was killed by the police in the course of the robbery. It's not true and these officers have come with me so you'll know the truth."

"Who the fuck is Lester?" The Prince demanded angrily. Max gave him a hard look. No swearing in the gym.

"Screwloose's real name was Lester Judge," I managed to say, "he told me over by the heavy bag."

Everyone exchanged a puzzled look. Screwloose was Lester?

Jimmy Gannon continued, "Some of you know Billy Touissant. He was on the scene last night. Let him tell you what happened."

Billy stepped forward, took off his hat and placed it under his arm. "First of all let me say that I'm sorry Lester was killed last night but you should know the police did not shoot him."

"If the police didn't shoot him who did?" Antoine demanded.

"Lester was killed when the pistol he was carrying went off as he was trying to pull it out of his pants pocket. The bullet struck him in the leg, severed his femoral artery and he bled to death before we could get him help," Billy announced.

"You sayin' he shot hisself?" Antoine hissed.

The police captain, who identified himself as Captain Murphy, stepped forward. "It was an accident. No other shots were fired at the scene by the police or anyone else. His two accomplices were arrested without incident."

Silence smothered the room. Everybody stared at their feet or shuffled around until Teddy spoke up. "How do we know you guys are tellin' the truth?"

"I went to the morgue, fellah's," Jimmy Gannon offered. "I saw the body. I didn't want to but I wanted to be able to tell you I saw the leg wound. That was the only injury." Screwloose.

The anger which had filled the room only a short while before dissipated, replaced by sadness. Another shooting. Another death. Screwloose.

That evening's Lowell Sun trumpeted the headline, "LOWELL TEEN KILLED IN ROBBERY." The story contained the statements of witnesses, the liquor store clerk and the police. The story indicated an "accidental discharge of a firearm" killed Lester Judge, one of the robbers.

Later that week I overheard two guys talking at a table in Lefty's. The conversation went like this:

"Did you hear the cops shot a guy who was trying to rob Trucotte's Liquor?"

"Yeah, he didn't even have a gun. They just shot him anyway."             Screwloose

**"When the legend becomes fact, print the legend."**

"A true friend accepts who you are, but also helps you become who you should be."

-Troy Steven

# Chapter Four

## *TKO*

"Hey Ferrier! How 'bout I smash your face in?"

That's Jerry Kovac talking, (threatening me actually) in the lunchroom at Lowell High. I wasn't sure why Jerry wanted to smash my face in, but I was sure I wasn't going to let him.

Jerry was a big mouth and a bully and a whole lot of other colorful words I would grow more comfortable with as I got older. He was an oversized kid with a bulging belly and a bad attitude. I had seen him pick fights before, mostly with guys smaller than him. Now he had settled on me.

"What's your problem, Jerry? Pants too tight?" I wasn't afraid of this guy. I didn't want to fight him, sort of, but he was starting it.

Some of the other kids sitting near us in the lunch room laughed when I asked about Jerry's pants and this really put him over the top. He stormed over to where I was sitting with Teddy.

"You think you're funny?" His face was all red and he was trying to puff himself up. I looked at Teddy and smiled. Teddy smiled back. He wasn't afraid of Jerry either.

"You done?" I asked as pleasantly as possible. Jerry wasn't done.

"How 'bout you meet me under the clock after school and I smash your face in?" Jerry seemed really determined about the face smashing thing.

"How 'bout we meet under the clock after school and see what happens next?" I replied.

"Three o'clock, Ferrier. You better be there." Jerry and his cronies stormed away.

"Don't start without me. See you at three," I said to their backs and went back to eating my sandwich. Teddy grinned, "What do you think that was all about?"

"Who knows? I didn't like that guy much before, now I like him even less and I didn't think that was possible."

Right about then Margaret Mary showed up from across the lunchroom where she had been sitting with her friends.

"What was that all about?" She asked sliding in next to me.

"Funny, Teddy just asked me the same question. I have no idea. Jerry seems to want to smash my face in."

Margaret Mary looked shocked. "Why?"

"Don't know, don't think I'll let him though."

I was not upset about this. The idea of fighting Jerry didn't scare me, and it didn't worry me. I would not have picked a fight with him, even though I thought he was a jerk, but now that he had started trouble with me I was fine with the idea. Fighting in Lowell was one way of getting status points. Tough guys were looked up to. Tough guys got in fights and I was just about over being The Guy Who Got Kicked Out Of Keith Academy. Besides, we were seniors now, the top of the ladder at Lowell High School. Those afternoons and Saturday mornings at Nelson's Gym were about to pay off.

"I don't want you to fight him, David. He's bigger than you." Margaret Mary's concern was genuine and it felt good to hear.

"Bigger don't mean better, Mags. Dave will take him easy." This vote of confidence from Teddy.

"I don't want him to take anybody. He could get hurt." More concern, much appreciated.

"I'm not going to start anything, but I'm meeting him under the clock after school. If he doesn't want to fight we won't. I promise."

Margaret Mary seemed relieved at this, but still worried.

"Besides," I added, "last time I met somebody under the clock he wanted to ask you out. How do you feel about Jerry?"

Margaret Mary rolled her eyes and stood up. She did not think I was funny. Sometimes I was funny though.

"Only two things can happen if you fight with Jerry. You could get hurt, which I don't want, or you could hurt him and I don't believe you want to be the type of person who hurts other people." Margaret Mary had a point. But he started it.

"Teddy, you're his friend, talk some sense into him." Then she walked away.

"Hit him hard, and often," Teddy said in a low voice so Margaret Mary wouldn't hear. I nodded my head and finished my lunch.

Three o'clock rolled around and I was under the clock at 3:08. Teddy was with me and a pretty good crowd had formed. Jerry and his buddies strode up.

"You ready Ferrier?" Jerry snorted.

"Just say where and when. Right now would be good."

We couldn't fight under the clock. We'd both get suspended if we did.

"Kitteridge, unless you're chicken," Jerry announced.

Kitteridge Park was nearby and the traditional stomping grounds for such activities.

"Let's go." Teddy and I started off for Kitteridge. A sizable crowd of students followed. When we got there I put my books and jacket on a bench and waited for Jerry to step up.

While I waited, Butchie, now Kevin, came over. Kitteridge park was Butchie's home court. It was across the street from his house, he did his roadwork there, his sister played there.

"Why you fighting this guy?" He asked.

"Don't know really. He wanted to fight me." My answer sounded stupid even as I said it. Butchie, now Kevin, snorted and walked over to Jerry.

"What's this fight about?" Even Jerry had enough sense to drop the bluster when he talked to Butchie.

"Ferrier called me a big fat idiot."

Butchie, now Kevin, motioned me over to where he and Jerry were standing.

"Did you call this guy a big fat idiot?" Butchie, now only Butchie, asked.

"I never said that, Butch," I answered.

"You say anything like that?" He added.

"Butchie, I never talk about Jerry at all and I didn't call him anything." I was telling the truth and Butchie, now Butchie, knew it.

"Donna Delancey told me you did!" Jerry proclaimed.

Butchie and I exchanged a look. Butchie had recently broken up with Donna, adding his name to the list of ex-boyfriends she was mad at. I was at the top of that list.

"I believe Dave, Jerry, but if you two want to fight, go ahead. I got the winner."

Now Jerry and I exchanged a look. I sure didn't want to fight Butchie, neither did Jerry.

"What do you mean Butchie?" I asked.

"My park, my rules. I fight the winner."

"I don't want to fight you Butch," Jerry added.

"Don't win." And Butchie, not Kevin, took off his jacket, walked over to the bench and waited. I decided to have a word with Jerry.

"Look Jerry, I didn't say anything like that to Donna Delancey or anybody else. I think she made it up so you would get mad at me. So that's a pretty stupid reason for us to fight. An even stupider reason is the winner has to get creamed by Butchie."

"I sure don't want to fight Butchie," Jerry concluded.

"How 'bout we shake on it and forget the whole thing?" I said.

I stuck out my hand. Jerry shook it. Butchie, now Kevin, put his shirt back on. Teddy handed me my jacket and books and we left Kitteridge Park. Jerry left with his buddies. Butchie, now Kevin, went to Brigham's and met Margaret Mary, who, I was later told, gave him a grateful kiss on the cheek.

*I've got sunshine on a cloudy day,*

*When it's cold outside,*

*I've got the month of May.*

*I guess you'd say,*

*What can make me feel this way?*

*My Girl, Talkin' about My Girl.*

**-Smokey Robinson**

And she didn't even know it yet.

<u>"My Girl"</u>, written by Smokey Robinson, recorded by the Temptations. Released December, 1964. Reached #1 on the Billboard Charts.

"True love stories never have endings."

**-John M.**

# Chapter Five

## *The Girl I Never Made Love To*

T'was the week before Christmas, in the Yuletide portion of the winter of 1964. The holiday season found us halfway through our Senior Year in High School with graduation looming big as a mountain just over the horizon. Year end tests had been taken, mid term report cards graded and distributed, and our classes were shutting down a full week before Santa came to town.

The year had passed in a blur. Weeks passed in order, rapidly, as the months changed and the calendar pages fluttered by.

Only last month Lyndon Baines Johnson had won over 60% of the popular vote and been elected (or re-elected if you didn't count how he became president in the first place) over his Republican rival, Barry Goldwater. The simmering, slowly escalating unrest in a far away country named Vietnam had been a glowering campaign issue. The Republican candidate, Barry Goldwater spoke for "the Hawks" the faction favoring increased US involvement in Vietnam's civil war. LBJ cloaked himself as a "Dove", the faction opposing our involvement in an overseas conflict. In October, during the heated presidential campaign, LBJ stated with great conviction, "We are not about to send American boys 9 or 10 thousand miles away from home to do what Asian boys ought to be doing for themselves." He said this despite quietly dispatching five thousand Marines to Vietnam eight weeks earlier bringing the total U.S. military presence in Vietnam to twenty-one thousand. This number was going to go up, way up. Johnson's peace platform promise was that it would not. And the peace candidate prevailed.

Teddy, prophetically, didn't believe him. "That guy looks like a crook to me." We'd see.

Also that year Martin Luther King had won the Nobel Peace Prize despite being labeled "the most notorious liar in the country" by J. Edgar Hoover, autocratic head of the FBI.

A controversial comedian by the name of Lenny Bruce was continuously arrested for using obscene language in his night club act. Mr. Bruce insisted on his right to freedom of speech, but he was arrested anyway and often.

And only last week Bob Hope announced he would be taking his USO entertainment program to South Vietnam for the first time to entertain our troops spending their Christmas overseas. Bless his heart forever.

Closer to earth, our earth anyway, was the imminent annual Immaculate Conception CYO Ski trip. Scheduled pre-Christmas this year we were to be off to Stowe, Vermont for the weekend, Friday, Saturday and return Sunday evening. There were 36 numbered cabins strewn around a frozen lake and a huge ski lodge fronting the ski slopes. As seniors we could choose the lodge or a cabin. Two to a cabin, boys and girls inflexibly separated, of course. I chose a cabin with Paul Sanders as my roommate. Teddy, couldn't come on the trip, he wasn't Catholic enough, or at all really. I had forgiven Paul, sort of, for kissing Margaret

Mary on last year's trip and he was now taking his turn dating Donna Delancey. And that is where the Great Plan began.

"So when Donna comes over you have to leave, right?" Paul outlined the plan. Paul knew about Donna and I from the past of course, but such things didn't seem to bother him. The rest of the plan was for me to sneak over to Margaret Mary's cabin after Linda Rogers snuck over to Peter Rayburn's cabin and so on. It was like checkers, only with hormone driven teenagers.

The jumping was set to commence after the 11PM Friday night curfew when the chaperones had settled in by the large stone fireplace in the main lodge for hot buttered rum and self-congratulations for a job well done. We'd see about that as well.

So soon after a cheerful good-night and an obedient, sincere response from us, the chaperones departed and the cabin hopping began. Donna arrived at our cabin minutes after the chaperone left, skirting past me without a word. I bundled up and skulked through the shadows to Margaret Mary's cabin.

A light snow had begun to fall turning the moonlight all silvery and coating the trees and rooftops of the lake cabins. I quickly located Margaret Mary's cabin and sneaked inside.

When I arrived Linda Evans had already left, off to her rendezvous with Peter Rayburn. Margaret Mary closed the door behind me with a hush and we stood in the candlelight and lantern not sure of what we should do next. For just a moment we watched our breath form steamy puffs in the frigid cabin. It seemed the candles and lantern were the sole sources of heat as well as light. Rustic, I think they call it. Colder than Nelson's Gym is how it felt.

I loved Margaret Mary with all the devotion, passion and sincerity a high school senior could muster. I felt that she loved me too, though we had never used those words. Though we had heard them, over and over, in our playlist of rock & roll fantasies, both of us knew in our hearts LOVE was serious business, deeper, by far then puppy love, infatuation or the ever evolving teenage crushes that surrounded us. While The Beatles! shouted "Yeah, Yeah, Yeah!" after announcing "She Loves You" and assured us "Money Can't Buy Me Love" and added "P.S. I Love You" to our playlist, the word had become more lyrical than meaningful. Margaret Mary recognized that love was a matter of considerable gravity, a matter of honesty and precision, not merely an impulse to be sung about. For myself the matter was more one of uncertainty and fear of the consequences of laying my heart so bare.

"You can put your hat and coat over there," Margaret Mary said indicating a high backed wooden chair in the corner. I thought she sounded a little nervous, which was exactly how I felt. She was dressed in a puffy-white, Christmassy-looking pullover sweater and shiny black ski pants with multi-buckled boots. Under my hat and coat I wore my CYO basketball sweater and jeans. The sneakers on my feet were not the best choice for traveling in snow. Under my arm I had a paper bag stuffed with my pajamas, a brown checkered woolen outfit which had appeared under last year's Christmas tree. And that you see was what the mutual nervousness was all about.

Margaret Mary and I had never slept together before. Certainly never had sex, at least not the intercourse variety. We had hugged and kissed, danced slow and fast, put our heads on each other's shoulders and held hands often and everywhere. Sex, the advanced, Donna Delancey steaming variety, was not part of our relationship. We were both semi-devout Catholics, Margaret Mary certainly a shade more intense than I, but Catholics we were. Sins were sins, and sins were bad. Sex, most certainly the kind that took place in cabins when two unmarried people slept together was a sin, a Big Sin, according to all we had been taught and come to believe. And friends, very good friends, as Margaret Mary and I most assuredly were, did not commit Big Sins with one another.

I piled my coat and hat on the chair and turned to face Margaret Mary. We looked at each other. Neither of us looked at the bed.

"What do you want to do?" I asked, avoiding as much responsibility as I could.

"I want to talk to you, David. I am frightened about this and not sure we should be doing it." Margaret Mary spoke, as she always did with an honesty and genuineness I had not yet mastered. She crossed to the bed and sat on the edge. There was nowhere else to sit in the room, except for the chair I had just piled my hat and coat on. I went to the bed and sat beside her. She took my hand in hers and I immediately felt and knew everything was going to be alright.

"What if I became pregnant? Margaret Mary said in a tiny, uncertain voice. I answered immediately, more bluster than confidence.

"If you did we could get married." Which I knew was not the solution to that problem.

"I don't want to get married, David. Not yet. I want to go to college next year, maybe become a teacher like my father, maybe become something else I haven't even thought of yet, but I couldn't do any of that if I had, we had, a baby."

Of course she was right. A thousand per cent right. As always.

"Well then we shouldn't do it then," I stammered, "Have sex I mean." I was blushing as red as Santa Claus' coat.

Margaret Mary turned to look at me. She moved closer on the bed and asked, "Did you ever have sex with Donna Delancey?"

Now I was redder than Santa's outfit. I answered honestly.

"No, not, "all the way" sex. Donna called it "pretend sex." But I don't think we ought to do that either," I added hurriedly, achieving a whole new stratosphere of redness as I squirmed away from Margaret Mary.

This somehow produced a muffled laugh, then a big, grateful, relieved, happy smile from Margaret Mary. She could see how uncomfortable I had become and I'm sure my face looked like it was on fire.

"David", she began, "You and I should never have "pretend" anything. I am not ready to have sex, but if I was it would be with you." She squeezed my hand and snuggled closer to me. Her head was on my chest and I put my arm around her shoulder. We sat like that for several moments, not saying anything as my skin color returned to normal and the nervousness I felt all night disappeared.

After a time Margaret Mary stood up and announced she was going to get ready for bed. She said I should too and took herself off to the tiny bathroom. I shucked my sneakers and jeans, traded my basketball sweater for my pajama top and stepped into the matching pants. Leaving my outdoor outfit on the floor I crossed to the bed and slid beneath the covers. A few minutes later Margaret Mary emerged from the bathroom wearing a full length, chin to toenails white woolen nightgown. Her red hair was brushed out, framing her face and falling to her shoulders. She had never looked so beautiful. She crossed to the bed and slid in beside me. We lay still for a moment, inches apart. Then she moved closer to me and I to her. Raising up on one elbow I clicked off the bedside lamp. I lay back in the darkness, everlastingly close to her, secure in the feelings we had for each other and the surety that good friends do not commit big sins together.

*And the fire is slowly dyin',*

*And, my dear, we're still goodbyin'*

*But as long as you love me so,*

*Let it snow, Let it snow,*

*Let it snow!*

<u>"Let It Snow!"</u>, Written by Sammy Kahn and Julie Styne. First performed by Vaughn Monroe (with the Norton Sisters) in 1945. A perennial which reached #1 for five weeks upon release.

# Chapter Six

## *Testing 1, 2, 3*

"These tests are important, David. We have to prepare for them."

Margaret Mary was in her all too familiar teacher/scolding mode as I slackered my way through a college board study session on her front porch.

"Important for what? I don't even know if I want to go to college," I answered, balancing surly with genuine confusion.

School had become a bore to me, a drudgery of memorizing information and repeating it back on tests. Subjects, such as literature and history, which allowed me to dig a little deeper than the facts to be memorized, still fascinated me, the rest, not at all. However that was the system, and the system had to be followed. So we were told.

"Important for your future," Margaret Mary said, balancing frustration with caring, a trait I recognized and cherished in her. "High school is going to be over soon. What are you going to do then?"

Good question. I wish I had a clue. All of our teachers told us over and over again how important it is to go to college and how important the College Entrance Exams are in making that possible. That is why I was on Margaret Mary's front porch this Tuesday evening when I could have been home watching "Combat!" on TV.

"I could get a job. My Uncle Artie said I could work for him over at the box factory."

Margaret Mary rolled her eyes in that especially exasperated way she had when she was really disappointed in me.

"Really? That's what you want to do? Make boxes?" She replied.

"I don't know!" (I really didn't). My Dad and Mom said I should make up my mind and do what I think is best. They said if I wanted to go to college they'd pay for it. But college costs a lot of money and I don't know if they can afford it."

"There are scholarships," Margaret Mary answered, "You are smart, you could get a scholarship. That's why we have to prepare for these exams."

This made sense, of course, but Margaret Mary almost always made sense.

"College is just more school. I'm sick of school. I want to get a job, earn some money, maybe buy my own car."

"And do what?" Margaret Mary was getting steamed. So was I. "Drive your car to your job making boxes for the rest of your life?"

This "rest of my life" business was getting more frightening all the time. Truthfully, I was more than a little scared to think about it. Up till now decisions had largely been made for me. Seventh grade led to eighth grade, freshman year to sophomore, but now, senior year to what? This time I was getting advice, not directions. More new ground.

"College is an option. If you don't do well on these tests you won't have that option."

She was right, of course. I knew that. Grateful for her insistence, we opened our books to study.

I have to tell you I am pretty good at the reading and history and vocabulary subjects and I could hold my own with geography, spelling, stuff like that, but Math, I don't know, something went wrong. I could add, subtract, divide and multiply with the best of them, but after that, nothing. Here's what I mean. Margaret Mary read me the first problem in the math section of our study guide. It went like this:

If $10x + 2 = 7$, what is the value of $2x$?

Seriously, I didn't have a clue. Totally blank. I could vaguely recall working such problems in math class, very vaguely. Mostly I just memorized whatever the teacher told us was the right answer and moved along from there.

"Go ahead, David, work it out," Margaret Mary offered.

She might as well have been asking a dog to play the piano. I stared straight ahead, sighed and shook my head.

Margaret Mary, only slightly exasperated explained, "It's easy, see, if ten somethings plus two equals 7, those ten somethings must be the number five because only five plus two equals seven, right?"

I nodded my head, the dimmest glimmer of understanding glowing through the fog.

"Now, if ten somethings equals five, what would one something be?" She waited patiently for my answer. So did I. The silence grew.

"One tenth of five!" She announced, patiently. "Now what is one tenth of five?"

The inner candle flickered. No words emerged. I stared at Margaret Mary. She stared at me. Doubt crossed her features as confusion ruled mine.

"Decimals, remember decimals," She hinted.

A decimal was a tenth. I remembered that. Ten times what equals five? Point 5 (0.5) emerged from my bewilderment. If one something (x) was worth 0.5, and you multiplied that by ten you get five. So one something (x) was 0.5, two somethings equaled 1.0.

"One," I triumphantly exclaimed. "Two x equals one!" The light came on in the dark room of my brain. Margaret Mary beamed satisfaction at my arrival at the answer she had formulated five long minutes ago. Unfortunately the light in my head dimmed as Margaret Mary read the next question.

"Solve for x, $12/24 = 10/x$."

I wrote the problem down on my pad. Once again I had no idea how to proceed. What was all this x nonsense? When would I ever need to know this garbage? The inner light winked out.

Just then Sean Patrick emerged from the house. He was carrying a tea tray with pot and cups and sugar cookies. I felt like I had been rescued from a fire.

"And how is it going, young scholars?" He asked, setting down the tray. "I thought perhaps some refreshments might be in order."

It was good to see Sean Patrick looking so healthy. He had been off the whiskey over four months now. He was attending a 12 step recovery program every week night at St. Joseph's church and on Saturday Margaret Mary went with him to a family meeting. His eyes were clear, his smile returned. He was back to teaching school, working on his book of poetry, glowing in Margaret Mary's life.

But all that was not the only reason I was so glad to see him. I put down my pad and reached for the teapot, eager to pour. Eager actually to do anything besides try to solve for x.

When I had filled each of our cups I passed Sean my notepad and asked, "Did you ever have to study this stuff, Mr. Sullivan?"

Sean glanced at my math scribble and smiled a mischievous smile.

"Ah, the equations, such as they are. Devilish things. Yes, I did, though they are well put behind me." Sean sipped his tea  and looked to Margaret Mary.

"And would you, daughter, be knowing this? He indicated the problem I had scribbled on my pad.

"'X' equals twenty," She replied immediately, decisively. I had no idea what she was talking about.

Sean nodded. I tried to look like I, of course, agreed. But I had a burning question.

"Did you ever have to actually use any of this stuff in your life, Mr. Sullivan? All this x equals something. What's it for?"

"Faith be told, if I told you I know for sure. But this much I have figured out. There is logic to be learned here. Logic in how things and situations can relate to one another when that relationship is not entirely obvious. Analytical thinking, such as it is called. Math, advanced math, is to my understanding the study of logic, of the breakdown of elements, or problems into factors which are more simple, and easier to understand."

"Mathematics is exercise for the brain," Margaret Mary added, repeating something she had undoubtedly read about in a book. "It's not just about finding out what x is, it's about finding out how to find what x is." She smiled appearing very satisfied with her answer. So did Sean. So did I, sort of.

"Are you knowing what our distinguished friend Albert Einstein himself said of mathematics?" Sean asked.

Margaret Mary and I leaned forward for the answer.

"He said, "Pure mathematics is, in its way, the poetry of logical ideas.""

Wow, I thought. Maybe if I could start to see this stuff as poetry I would begin to understand it, even like it. Fat chance so far.

"Mathematics is about thinking, David," Margaret Mary offered. "It's about figuring things out which aren't obvious at first sight. Math trains your brain to think."

Where she got this information I had no idea, however she seemed very sure of it and that was good enough for me. I reconsidered the "x" problem and could see, after some mental squinting how "x" would equal twenty. "Twenty is two times ten and twenty-four is two times twelve, right?" I semi-guessed.

"Yes!" Margaret Mary beamed. Sean smiled and sipped his tea.

"Mathematics is only one part of the exam, David," Margaret Mary reminded, "You will do very well on the reading comprehension and vocabulary, general knowledge parts, but you have to study mathematics or your scores won't be high enough to get you into a good college."

"It's sure I am you'll both fare well in the coming testing," Sean said. "And where would you be thinking of attending college my lad?" Sean asked.

And I truly had no answer. Outside of my wavering over whether or not I wanted to go to college at all was the fact that I was of the opinion that college chose you rather than you choose a college.

"Wherever they will take me I guess," was the best answer I could conjure.

Margaret Mary did a semi-subtle eye roll, Sean leaned forward. "Perhaps that is the wrong question. What is it you would like to study once a college accepts you?" He asked.

I couldn't answer. Silence built until I realized I really needed to know, and choose a path here. So far school had been drifting, doing what I was told as I was told to do it. Like I said before, memorize and repeat. Like training a parrot.

"I, I don't know." And to my embarrassment I truly didn't. Till Margaret Mary once again, came to my rescue.

"You are a good writer, David. You always get the highest marks on your papers and the stories you make up are really good."

I squirmed a bit here. Margaret Mary was the only person I had ever shown the stories I made up. Cowboy tales, right from the York Beach campfires, a few ghosts and goblins, and sports tales stolen directly from Chip Hilton.

"You are a writer then lad?" Sean said. "This does not surprise me. A good reader almost always make a good writer."

"And you are the only person I know who reads as much as me," Margaret Mary added. "You should study journalism, take a lot of English courses, learn to be an author."

I was more than taken aback by this turn of conversation. I had never, ever, spoken of how much I wanted to be a writer to anyone, even Margaret Mary. She knew, of course, how much I liked writers like Mark Twain for everything, Edgar Rice Burroughs for his wonderful Tarzan and John Carter stories, Zane Grey for the cowboys and Clair Bee for the Chip Hilton sports books gifted to me by my most wonderful aunt, Eileen.

Margaret Mary had visited upon me loftier editions, Victor Hugo for the fantastic adventures, Charles Dickens for the Christmas Carols, Ralph Ellison for the social awakening, Langston Hughes for the poetry.

Books were my cornerstone, second only to TV, which was my narcotic. But books were gaining fast. I mean after a while we all knew Matt Dillon was not going to get killed in Dodge City, same for Paladin, Cheyenne Bodie, Sugarfoot and all the other TV cowpokes I watched week after week. And no matter how many Nazis, tanks, bombs or battleships Sergeant Saunders or Lieutenant Hanley faced on Combat, they were going to be back next week. Cops were always going to vanquish, Good Guys would always prosper, Bad Guys never won. At least on TV.

"A writer then is what my good daughter sees in you," said Sean, "then a writer you should consider being, as she is seldom wrong in such opinions."

Margaret Mary smiled. Sean smiled. I gulped. A door had opened. A secret dream was becoming an actual possibility.

"You really think I could become a writer?" I asked while asking myself.

"Of course you could, David." Margaret Mary squeezed my arm. Hope and inspiration squeezed my heart.

"And wouldn't you be yet another great writer from our fair city of Lowell, liken to our own Mr. Kerouac, blessed may he be," Sean added.

I had heard, somewhat vaguely of Lowell's own Jack Kerouac, though he was far from a favorite son or even a local celebrity. He had written a famous book I had never read called "On The Road," and I had come to understand it had something to do with being a beatnik or a drug addict, I wasn't sure which. I did know that there was little local mention or acclaim for him however and for the first time I began to wonder why.

"Is Jack Kerouac a good writer, Sean?" I asked.

"He has the heart of an Irishman for sure, though he writes with the passion of the Francais, even though he was raised in our own Centerville."

Centerville was a working class section of Lowell marked by three story tenements, ten stool street corner bars and eight table diners. The roads were crowded and small, the cars battered and seldom new, and all of the houses looked like they had been painted on the same day, many, many years ago.

"Jack Kerouac is from Centerville?" I played baseball in Centerville and had never heard his name mentioned.

"He was indeed," Sean replied, "Have you not read his book?"

As I shook my head no Margaret Mary left the room. I knew where she was going and what she was coming back with.

"A fine writer he is," Sean continued, "though like myself he is cursed with the whiskey. Would you like to hear a wee bit of what he has written?"

This he said as Margaret Mary reappeared holding, you guessed it, a well worn copy of "On The Road." Sean thumbed the pages as Margaret Mary settled in next to me.

"Here it is," Sean said, holding the book before him. "Here is a bit of what should be in the heart of all who wish to write of things that matter." He began reading…

*"the only ones for me are the mad ones, the ones who are mad to live, mad to be saved, desirous of everything at the same time, the ones who never yawn or say a common place thing, but burn, burn, burn, like fabulous yellow roman candles exploding like spiders across the stars and in the middle you can see the blue center light pop and everybody goes, 'Awww…'"*

Sean clapped the book closed as the words echoed in my ears.

Those were the ones I wanted to know! To be with, to burn with, to go 'Awww' with! This guy Jack Kerouac had written about what I secretly dreamed of, but knew not how to express. And he was from Lowell! Just like me!

This, to me, made the world feel like it had more possibilities, like I had more…permission. This was a passion shared, a dream defined.  All I had to do was find out how to get there.

"Can I borrow that book?" I exclaimed as Sean held it out to me.

"Now you know what to read," Margaret Mary suggested, "but now we should get back to how you can learn more about writing."

She was right of course. Smug, but right anyway.

So we spent the next hour solving for x and y and different sorts of angles and hypotenuses. Sean stayed with us, coaching and encouraging as the tea became cold in the cups and the math began to come a bit easier to me. After I had successfully worked out the volume of a rectangular box I sat back triumphantly and smiled.

"How's that for poetry?" I beamed.

Margaret Mary laughed her very special laugh and Sean rose to go back in the house.

"I shall leave you two to continue your studies. Good on you for the effort. I am sure success will follow. And I felt good, pleased at my efforts, grateful for the help I was receiving. Just good all over.

Margaret Mary leaned forward and turned the page of the study guide before us. Pointing to a problem she said, "Okay, try this one."

"Find the length of the hypotenuse of a right triangle whose legs are 5cm and 12cm."

No wonder Jack Kerouac went On The Road.

**"A child without education is like a bird without wings."**

-Tibetan Proverb

Don't know much about history,

Don't know much biology,

Don't know much about a science book,

Don't know much about the

French I took.

But I do know that I love you,

And I know that if you love me too,

What a wonderful world it would be.

Don't know much about geography,

Don't know much trigonometry,

Don't know much about algebra,

Don't know what a slide rulers for.

But I do know that I love you,

And I know that if you love me too,

What a wonderful world it would be.

"What A Wonderful World It Would Be", Written by Sam Cooke, Herb Alpert and Lou Adler. Recorded by Sam Cooke, Released in April, 1964. Reached #12 on the Billboard charts. Re-released in 1978 after being featured in the film, "Animal House" and reached # 2 on the charts.

1965
THE Spindle

# Chapter Seven

## *Graduation Blues*

The high school-senior, end of year deadlines were flying by. First, each of us graduating seniors had to go to Loring Studios to have our class picture taken before April 1. Dress code was jacket and tie for boys, closed collar for girls. Hair neat and trimmed. No exceptions.

Then there was the whole class ring procedure. The way this worked was you went to Scott Jewelers in Kearney Square (down-city) and got measured for your ring. Then you had to put a ten dollar deposit on the ring. After that you could pay fifty cents a week until the balance of $22.50 was paid. Class rings would be distributed on May 15th to all graduating seniors (who were paid up).

Those tasks accomplished, I was measured for a boys blue cap and gown, filled out a biography card for the class of 1965 yearbook, "The Spindle" and attended not one, but two rehearsals for the graduation ceremony to be held at Cawley Memorial Stadium on Sunday afternoon, June 15th, 1965.

There was a Senior Prom, of course. White sport coat and a pink carnation for Teddy and I. I attended with Margaret Mary who was beautiful in a peach colored gown Teddy described, in a good way, as looking like really fancy toilet paper. Teddy's date, Janet Sikouras, wore a red dress which could only be described as "Wow!" and nearly got her sent home to change. Cooler heads prevailed, corsages and bouquets were bandied about and the Lowell High School Dance Band played "Moon River" about ten times throughout the temporarily unforgettable evening.

High school was ending. The future beckoned. I was scared as hell.

"I'm joinin' the Marines, just like Chris," Teddy announced as we walked home from school after our final day of classes.

"Teddy, are you sure that's a good idea? That last letter you read us from Chris sounded like he was having a really bad time," Margaret Mary answered with some concern. I could only nod my head in agreement.

Chris' last letter had spoken rather cryptically about things getting worse and not better where he was. That somewhere was near or around a far away place called Da Nang, Republic of South Vietnam. The Marines, we learned, were involved in heavy fighting there. Chris was with those Marines.

The television news droned ominously about "increased guerilla activity" and solemnly referred to "growing U.S. casualties" in the Southeast Asian conflict. Student demonstrations against the war were sprouting up on college campuses across the country. And, after an attack on one of our Naval vessels, the USS Maddox, in a place called the Gulf of Tonkin, Congress had hurriedly passed a bill called the Southeast Asia Resolution Act. This bill gave President Johnson the power to do whatever he felt was necessary to stop the

"Communist aggression" in Southeast Asia without consulting Congress, or anyone else. The "dove in the White House" was changing his feathers.

Only two US Senators opposed this "war powers" bill. One, Ernest Gruening, a Democrat from the state of Arkansas, stated his objection to, "sending our American boys into combat in a war in which we have no business, which is not our war, into which we have been misguidedly drawn and is steadily being escalated."

Which sounded remarkably like a campaign promise Lyndon Johnson had made, and apparently forgotten, when he ran for president last fall.

Immediately after the resolution's passage the Pentagon began demanding US troop strength in Vietnam be increased from its present 23 thousand to 175 thousand. LBJ, of course, signed off, and the draft quotas for eighteen year olds, (like we would be in a very short time) increased from 17 thousand (a month) to 35 thousand! ( a month). My math may not have been the greatest but even I could figure out that amounted to over 350 thousand eighteen year old boys going into the army and then going somewhere else. The times they were indeed a-changin'.

Meanwhile our rock & roll radio was broadcasting an ominous song by a guy named Barry McGuire which had these lyrics:

*The eastern world, it is explodin',*

*Violence flaring, bullets loadin',*

*You're old enough to kill,*

*But not for votin,*
*You don't believe in war,*
*But what's that gun you're totin?*

The song was called "Eve of Destruction". It goes on to proclaim:

*Take a look around you boy, it's bound to*
*scare you boy,*
*And you tell me over and over again,*
*How you don't believe*
*We're on the Eve Of Destruction.*

Songs like this were popping up all over Top 40 radio stations, sandwiched between mind worms like "Wooly Bully", "I Got You Babe" and "Mrs. Brown You've Got a Lovely Daughter." When yodeling poet Bob Dylan asked,

*How many times must the cannonballs fly*
*Before they are forever banned?*

He told us the answer was "Blowin' In The Wind".

We were suddenly a long way from "Blue Suede Shoes", "Hound Dog", and even, "I Want To Hold Your Hand". Folk music, as they called it was on the rise. Singing groups like The Kingston Trio, Peter, Paul and Mary, and The New Christy Minstrels, crooned alongside solo performers like Joan Baez, Tom Rush and Buffy St. Marie extolling not "Be

Boop A Lula" but chanting about social issues, racial equality and smoldering wars. Rock and Roll was growing up, as were we.

The Beatles! of course, were still around giving us, "No Reply", "I'm A Loser", She's A Woman" and Chuck Berry's, "Rock and Roll Music". The British Invasion was at its peak with plenty of bubblegum music to hum around in our heads. But as cheerful as all this was, long time balladeer Pete Seeger questioned, "Where Have All the Flowers Gone?" and further added,

*Where have all the young men gone?*

*Gone for soldiers every one.*

*When will they ever learn?*

*When will they ever learn?*

Rock and Roll, our musical conscience, was changing along with our social awareness and the social consequences.

So far this year, quietly, without fanfare or significant public notice, over a thousand US troops, mostly teenagers like ourselves, had been killed in Vietnam. That number would almost double by the end of the year.

"Chris is a corporal now," Teddy continued, "He's with the 9th Marines, the toughest fighting guys in the world. That's what I want to be too."

Teddy's announcement hung there, in the early summer air, like a farewell and a foreboding.

"I think it will all be over pretty soon Teddy," I hoped as I replied, "The news says we're sending a lot more guys over there to finish 'em off."

"My father says wars are not won by the numbers of soldiers fighting but by the commitment of their leaders to victory." Margaret Mary was quoting Sean, as she often did. Would that we had understood.

"Of course we're gonna' win," Teddy responded. "We always win."

"Well, I hope we win before you have to go over there," Margaret Mary added. "And I hope nobody else we know has to go over there either," She proclaimed, aiming a meaningful glance at me.

Two months ago I had been accepted as a freshman at Suffolk University in Boston. Suffolk was primarily a law school but they had a very good school of journalism as well. I had been accepted not entirely based on my grades but on their reaction to a short story I had written in high school that Margaret Mary insisted I include in my application packet.

Around Christmas time I had written the story for a correspondence school I saw advertised in a magazine that had a picture of the Twilight Zone guy, Rod Serling, smoking a cigarette of course, saying if I passed an Aptitude Test, which I could take for free, the Famous Writers School would teach me how to be a Famous Writer. I sent for the test and mailed it back to them along with my short story.

I told Margaret Mary, of course, and showed her my story. She showed it to Sean, and they both said it had Promise.

Promise was something people were always telling me I had. Figuring out how to live up to that promise was the part that had me worried most.

"My aunt Rose said I could live with her this fall when I start my classes," Margaret Mary said as we walked along, chatting about our future.

Margaret Mary had been accepted at Loyola University in Chicago where her father used to teach. She planned to take Humanities courses for her first year or so before choosing a professional path. As always she had given her future a lot of thought and made plans to accomplish her goals.

Living with Aunt Rose would mean goodbye for me and Margaret Mary, just as the Marine Corps would mean goodbye for me and Teddy. There was a lot to this graduation business that was a lot more scary than fun. The future was a vast unknown that for me was less frightening if I had my friends with me. Friends who were planning their goodbyes.

"You gonna' live in Boston when you're at Suffolk?" Teddy asked.

But the expense was too much and I had agreed with my parents that commuting by train would be best and I would live at home.

"No," I answered, "Costs too much." I was staying in Lowell. Margaret Mary and Teddy were not.

"Well we have to keep in touch with each other. We can write letters and talk on the phone on weekends," Margaret Mary suggested.

"I don't think the Marines have weekends," Teddy replied. "But I will write. I promise."

Every sentence, every promise, made me feel worse. I was losing my two best friends. Life was changing. I was not. Suffolk University felt like something I was supposed to do, expected to do. College was not my choice, not yet. However I didn't have any other plan so college it may as well be.

Walking along our familiar sidewalks, passing the comfortable houses and the same streets, in the same order, suddenly felt lonely and sad. This was not the jubilee I was expecting when high school was finished.

Two days later we were lined up, alphabetically, segregated by boys and girls, of course, in our graduation caps and gowns to receive our high school diplomas. Graduation was no longer coming. It was here.

There was a lot of happiness after the ceremony. Handshakes and back slaps, cheek kisses and Hallmark cards, a cake, I was sure awaited. I took deep breaths, smiled a lot even when I saw Margaret May and Sean walk away together and Teddy going off with his father and sister. We would not be going off to school together any more. No more classes, no more lunch room. No more meeting under the clock as we ventured Onward.

## Postscript

About a month after I sent my test kit in, I received an answer back from Famous Writers School. They said I passed the test and they really liked my story. They also said it cost $750 to take their course to be a Famous Writer.

When I showed the whole package of information from Famous Writers School to my parents they were really proud, at first. They also thought $750 was a lot of money for a correspondence course. Margaret Mary and Sean thought so too. Teddy said it sounded crooked to him. I threw away the stuff from Famous Writers school but I kept my short story.

What I wrote:

# Battle Cry

## Short story by David O. Ferrier

The bullet deep in my chest was burning. I couldn't move my legs and the rest of my body felt cold and numb. I was lying in a grassy field. It was night. There were lots of stars in the sky. There were a lot of dead bodies around me. Some of them were my friends. Some had been my enemies.

A great battle had taken place here today. At least it felt like a great battle to those of us who were in it. I was very frightened as shells exploded around me and bullets made a whizzing sound as they flew past me. Then I was hit, knocked off my feet and thrown to the ground. It felt like I had been struck, very hard, by an unseen  hammer. Hollering men rushed past me, first forward, then backward in panicked retreat. I lay still, bleeding.

It was daytime when I was hit, early afternoon as I recall. Now it was night. I was no longer frightened. But I couldn't move, not much anyway. I tried to raise myself up and couldn't. My arms seemed to work and I could move my head. The blood around the hole in me was caked and hard but there was a lot of blood on the ground around me.

Far off I could hear sounds. Low sounds. Groans. Soft cries of pain. Hushed voices. They were getting further away. I tried to call out. My throat was dry and I could make no sound. The harder I tried the weaker I felt. I lay my head down on the ground and felt the fear returning.

Then I heard the horse. Coming toward me it seemed. Getting louder. Using all my strength I raised my head. To see. To maybe have someone see me. Not far off there was a gray horse, and there was a man on it. Moving very slow and heading right for me.

At first the figure on the horse was dim. He was wearing a slouch hat. His face hidden by the brim and the shadows. As he drew near I could make out his uniform. Gray, confederate gray. There was a scribble of gold braid on the sleeve, what looked like a sword dangling from the saddle. A rebel officer wandering the battlefield. Touring among the dead and dying. I reached for my pistol, snug in my holster, wet with my blood. As quietly as I could I drew my pistol. The rebel officer came closer. I managed to stretch the gun out in front of me and sight along the barrel. The pistol shook, my hands trembled. With a great effort I drew the hammer back and sighted on the horseman.

As he drew nearer I wondered what kind of man would ride this bloody ground after this bloody day. Though I could not see his face I imagined a smile, a victor's grin perhaps. I tightened my hold one the pistol and tried to squeeze the trigger. As I did I felt the blood begin to run wet once more from my wound. My head swam and the pistol was getting heavy. I was passing out. I imagined once again the victor's grin. The evil satisfaction. My strength returned. I steadied my hand.

As my finger tightened on the trigger the moonlight caught the face of the rider. I knew this man! Knew the face from a hundred photographs, newspaper stories, handbills which shouted, Traitor! Turncoat! Renegade! On the gray horse, moving slowly across the battleground toward me was General Robert E. Lee.

My finger tightened on the trigger. Hate filled my heart and fed my fading strength. And just as I felt the trigger begin to give, the man on the horse looked up. No victor's grin. No evil smile. He was crying. Crying in the moonlight as he rode past me. I lost my grip on the pistol. My breath ran ragged. And I cried as well as he passed by me into the night.

This was of course, the culmination of every comic book I had ever read up to that point. Bless 'em all.

"I never let my schooling get in the way of my education."

-Mark Twain

"I think any comic book or really any book you can read is an educational tool in that it helps literacy. The more you read, the better you get at it."

-Stan Lee

"There is a superhero in all of us, we just need the courage to put on a cape."

-Superman

# Chapter Eight

## *Letter To Teddy*

"A letter came for ya! It's from Chris!" I shouted as I ran across my front lawn to where Teddy was standing. Teddy's older brother, Chris, had disappeared, over the hill and far away about a year ago. He took off on his motorcycle for parts unknown after a series of arguments with Teddy's Dad. This was the first word from Chris since he left. The letter came to my house, addressed to Teddy care of me. I don't know why Chris mailed it that way, but he did, and I had It, and I couldn't wait to get it to Teddy, he's my buddy.

He froze in his driveway as I waved the red white and blue bordered envelope. The envelope was creased and battered and stained with a red dust. It looked like it had come from a long way away.

When I handed Teddy the envelope we both stared at the return address. It read:

LCPL C.D. Gianoulous 3141614

D-1-4, Third Marine Amphibious Force

C/O FPO San Francisco, Calif. 96601

"Third Marine Amphibious Force, that means Chris is in the Marines." I was still good at stating the obvious.

Teddy swallowed hard when I said that. He made no move to open the letter.

"Aren't you gonna' open it?" Happy as I was for Teddy I was very curious to hear what Chris had written.

"Um, not yet," Teddy answered, "I think I'll just hold on to it for a while."

Yeah, personal stuff. Margaret Mary would have known that right away. I was still learning.

"Okay, I'll see you later. Hope everything is all right." I went back to my house. When I closed the front door I could see Teddy standing in his driveway holding the unopened letter.

An hour or so later Teddy came over. He had the letter. It was open.

"Wanna hear what Chris wrote to me?"

"You bet," I answered. We went into the living room and sat on the sofa. My Mom came in and said hello to Teddy. She knew about the letter.

"You can read it out loud if you want," Teddy said as he passed me the envelope. My Mom wiped her hands on a dish towel and sat across from us. I started to read:

June 13, 1965

Hey Teddy,

I'm sorry I haven't written before, I've been moving around a lot, real busy. About eight months ago I joined the Marine Corps out in San Diego. I didn't want Dad to know so he wouldn't screw it up for me. You know I had to get out of there before something bad happened between him and me so here I am. I heard so much from him about how disappointed he was in me that I started being disappointed in myself. That's why I joined the Marines.

I hope you are all okay. Has Connie graduated from hairdresser school yet? I heard you knocked out a guy named Kid Gallavan from Tewksbury. When did you start boxing? You can write me back and tell me all about it if you want to.

I guess you want to know why I joined the Marine Corps. I picked them because they are the toughest. Well let me tell you that's the truth. Being a Marine is the best thing I have ever done in my life. Boot camp was hard, but I made it alright. After that I went to special weapons training and that was pretty tough as well. When we graduated our instructors told us we should be very proud to call ourselves Marines and I am.

I'm in a place called Da Nang in South Vietnam. I belong to the Third Marine Division. I'm a rifleman, part of a weapons squad which means I get to hump a lot of ammo for the BAR that's a Browning Automatic Rifle, kind of like a machine gun. Sounds like fun? Not so far.

It's hot over here day and night and humid, lots of jungle. The people are very poor and nobody is sure who the enemy is or where he is hiding. In the daytime the people look like a bunch of farmers but at night they snipe at us and try to blow us up. We go on patrols during the day and pull perimeter guard on an airfield at night.

A couple of the guys I came over here with have gotten killed already but we have killed a lot more VC on our patrols. I know this sounds bad but I am with the best fighting force in the world, the Marines, and I know how to take care of myself so don't worry.

There's a girl out in San Diego named Sandy Myers. She's taking care of my bike and stuff. If anything happens to me I want you to have my bike. You'll have to figure out how to get it back from San Diego. I gave her your address and Dave's so she can get in touch with you if anything happens.

Please tell Connie that I miss her and tell Dad I'm okay. I'll write to you when I can and I'll send the next letter to the house after you've broken the news. It's starting to get dark now and I have to get ready to go on perimeter guard.

You're a good kid, Teddy and I am proud that you're my little brother. I hope I can make you proud of me as a Marine.

Take care,
Chris

P.S. You can write me back at this address if you want.

I folded the letter and handed it back to Teddy failing to notice the look of concern on my mother's face.

"That's pretty cool, him being in the Marines and all," I said.

"Yeah, except what he said about guys getting killed that he knew and stuff." Teddy sounded worried.

"I wonder how he knew about your fight with Kid Gallavan?"

"Probably one of his friends told him. I bet Leo Skelton knew where he was all the time."

"Yeah, Leo is his buddy. You gonna' write him back?"

"Yeah, maybe you can like, help me, I don't want to sound dumb or nuthin'."

"You won't sound dumb, Teddy, just tell him how you feel and how happy you were to hear from him," My mother suggested.

"Should I tell Connie and my father about the letter, Mrs. Ferrier?" Teddy asked.

"Of course, Teddy. Don't you think they have been worried too?"

"Connie has, I don't know about my Dad," Ted answered.

"Well, he has, I'm sure of it. You should tell them as soon as they get home."

Teddy agreed and I walked with him over to his house. No one was home yet.

"You know who else we should tell? Margaret Mary. She could help you write a really good letter to Chris," I suggested.

Yeah, that's a really good idea." Teddy brightened. "Wanna' go over and see if she's home now?"

And we did, and she was, and we settled on her front porch, Margaret Mary, me, Teddy and the letter, which Teddy handed to her as soon as we were seated.

Margaret Mary took the letter, opened it carefully, in her special way, and began reading. Teddy and I fidgeted on our chairs.

"How do you feel about getting this letter, Teddy?" She asked after she passed the letter back.

"Kind of like glad, I guess, Teddy began, "but now I'm kinda' worried because of the guys getting killed and all."

"Well the newspapers say Vietnam is a dangerous place right now. But your brother is with the Marines and they go to dangerous places," Margaret Mary replied.

"I don't even know where Vietnam is," Teddy said.

"Me neither," I added.

"Want to see? I'll be right back."

Margaret Mary left the porch and went back into the house. Moments later she emerged carrying a book. There was always a book.

Margaret Mary placed a large World Atlas on the low coffee table in front of us. With a sure hand she turned the pages, then stopped and pointed to a small country on the coast of the South China Sea.

"There," she announced. "That is South Vietnam."

"Wow," Teddy exclaimed, "why would the Marines want to go way over there to fight guys?"

Teddy always knew how to ask the right questions.

"Last year two of our Navy ships were attacked by North Vietnamese gunboats here." Margaret Mary pointed again at the map, "in the Gulf of Tonkin. Then President Johnson ordered the Marines to go to Vietnam and help the South

Vietnamese people from being conquered by the communists."

"Just like when those Cuban guys tried to attack us before," Teddy added.

"Sort of," Margaret Mary replied, "although I'm not sure it's exactly the same."

"Communists are always attacking us," Teddy said.

"What do you think, David?" Margaret Mary asked.

"I remember what President Johnson said when he was running for President last year. We did a report on it remember?"

Margaret Mary nodded, not remembering.

"He said, 'We are not about to send American boys 9 or 10,000 miles away from home to be doing what Asian boys ought to be doing for themselves.' I remember because I wrote it down, it was in my report," I answered.

"It sounds like something President Kennedy would have said," Margaret Mary replied.

"Only he wouldn't have done it anyway," I added.

"If the communists are attacking somebody we're supposed to go help them," Teddy said. "That's why Chris is over there right now."

I sure hoped Teddy was right. So did Margaret Mary.

So a letter to Chris was put together. Not that afternoon, but the next, after Teddy had spoken with his sister and father. They were going to write to Chris too, but Teddy wanted his letter to be just from him. He really didn't need any help, but he used my very special pen and here is what Teddy wrote,

Hi Chris,

It was really great to hear from you. I'm glad you are alright and I'm really proud that you are a US Marine. I told Connie and Dad and let them read your letter. I hope you aren't mad at me for letting them read it. Connie got all teared up, like she always does, and Dad didn't say a lot but I think he got kind of teared up too. He's asked me a bunch of times if I've heard from you and always looked sad when I said no. He said he was going to write to you this weekend. So did Connie. Dad's been a lot different since you've been gone. He doesn't yell at me as much and lets me work with him down at the garage on Saturdays and Sundays. He even pays me too, five dollars an hour! That's more than Dave makes at Lefty's, but Dave gets to eat all he wants to.

I've been going to Nelson's Gym for about a year now. I didn't knock that guy Kid Gallavan out, I got a decision. It was my first fight, a three rounder. I've fought three more times since then, I got a TKO and two more decisions. I'm undefeated, just like Cassius Clay!

Everybody here is real worried about you being in Vietnam. Me too, but I know you are going to be alright. Please write to us a lot if you can. I know you are real busy but we will all feel better every time we hear from you. I'll write a lot too, if you don't mind.

You know how you wrote that Dad said he was always disappointed in you? I don't think he really was, Connie says he's just always sad and unhappy because Mom died. Besides, I know I never was disappointed in you, I thought you were the coolest guy in Lowell and I still do. I'm really proud you are my big brother and I don't want anything to happen to you so be careful, okay? Dave and Margaret Mary both say hello and Margaret Mary said she is going to light a candle down at her church every week until you get home. I thought that was real nice of her. I'm going to mail this now and I will write again as soon as something happens around here.

I hope I hear from you real soon, be careful,

Your proud brother,
Teddy.

I wasn't the only one who could write very special things with my very special pen set.

"We sleep safely at night because rough men stand ready to visit violence on those who would harm us."

**-Winston Churchill**

GREETINGS FROM
YORK
BEACH
MAINE

# Chapter Nine

## *York Beach Redux*

"So the ball is supposed to go in the clown's mouth, down that chute and out on to that little lawn where the hole is?" Margaret Mary asked with a combined sense of wonder and what the hell?

"Yes," I explained. "This is miniature golf. You said you wanted to play miniature golf, so here we are. Hit the ball into the clown's mouth!"

Margaret Mary rolled her eyes, swung her putter and laughed as she watched her ball bounce down the curved sidewalk next to the clown's mouth.

"Nice shot," I commented, master of sarcasm that I was becoming.

"We won't count that one. It was practice." Margaret Mary went to fetch her ball. I lined up my shot. Right down the sidewalk. Margaret Mary brought my ball back with hers. Practice. The smile on her face was totally worth the fifty cents price of admission.

I was proudly showing off downtown York Beach Maine to Margaret Mary on her first ever visit there. In all the summers my family had been coming to York, events and circumstances had never aligned for Margaret Mary to come with us. Now on this last weekend of summer, Labor Day, 1965 we were together, hitting colored golf balls into a clown's mouth. It was a postcard beautiful Saturday night, as Margaret Mary and I strolled around Animal Forest Park, the ages old Amusement Park and Petting Zoo, nestled in a brightly lit corner of downtown. Earlier that day we had shared a blanket on Long Sands Beach, ran and jumped and frolicked in the waves as Margret Mary gradually turned a slightly bright shade of red, with freckles. We left the beach in mid-afternoon and after dinner with my family took the family car to downtown York.

The clown gobbled up Margaret Mary's next putt and mine. After that we putted around the rest of the wonderful eighteen hole miniature golf course at Animal Forest Park. We played through a series of windmills, waterfalls, a pirate ship and loop de loops getting our full 50 cents worth of fun. I stopped keeping score after the fifth hole (I was winning) because Margaret Mary was the least competitive person I ever met and it was more fun just playing than playing to win.

After our round of mini-golf we rode the Wild Mouse, tromped through the Fun House, tilted on the Tilt-a-Whirl and, at Margaret Mary's insistence, rode the Merry-Go-Round, twice.

"Has it always been this much fun?" Margaret Mary asked as we sat on a park bench watching the Ferris Wheel go round and round.

"Always," I answered as I put my arm around her. She scooted closer as I continued, "When we were little kids we would come here as a family. We didn't always have a lot of money to spend on rides and treats but just walking around, just being here was always fun."

"Did you have a favorite ride?" She asked.

"The Wild Mouse, for sure." Which was a kind of mini-roller coaster with little cars that had mouse ears on them. It was far from the breathtaking seaside coasters at Salisbury Beach and Nantasket, but for York Beach, it was the best.

"Let's ride it again," She suggested, "before we leave."

And thought brought a melancholy moment of silence for both of us. When we left, tonight, it would not only be the end of summer. Our childhoods, in a very meaningful way, would be ending as well. In three days Margaret Mary was leaving Lowell to stay with her Aunt Rose in Hammond, Indiana as she started her freshman year at Loyola University. I would begin commuting, by train, into Boston to start my freshman year at Suffolk University. Peter Rayburn would be attending Boston College to study law. Teddy was going to work full time at the garage with his father. Butchie, now Kevin, had signed up for the Navy. Our gang was breaking up. The times they were a-changin'.

Earlier that evening we shared a grilled cheese sandwich and two lime rickeys in the dining room of the Goldenrod Candy Shoppe, a downtown York Beach landmark unchanged in all the years my family had been coming here. In the shoppe's large storefront window a bright and shiny taffy pulling machine twisted and stretched colorful strands of gooey taffy, then chopped them up into wax paper wrapped "Salt Water Taffy" kisses. There were peanut butter, peppermint, banana, maple sugar and orange cream kisses, chocolate and strawberry, even watermelon and cotton candy flavors. Enough to suck every tooth in your mouth out. But delicious.

Behind the long glass countertops of the Goldenrod candy counter mouth watering trays of home made fudge, Pistachio, Maple Walnut, Penuche, Chocolate (of course), Vanilla and Salted Caramel were cut into blocks and sold in white paper bags to eager crowds of vacationers. Like Margaret Mary and I. Clutching our white bags of fudge, Penuche for me, Pistachio for Margaret Mary, we strolled the streets of downtown York Beach. We looked in the windows of the gaily decorated beach wear stores, post card emporiums, t-shirt and sweatshirt clothiers, and sea shell shops.

We stopped to listen to the outdoor jukebox at the Fun-O-Rama penny arcade. "Walk. Don't Run" by the Ventures never sounded better along with "Runaround Sue", "Travelin' Man and "The Battle of New Orleans", tunes that jangled and swirled into the night air before drifting upward into the summer stars. Next to the arcade a ten lane bowling alley offered candlepin bowling on lanes often slowed by drifting beach sand. Wooden pins clacked and flew about in the night combining with the next door penny arcade rock and roll jukebox in a symphony only found in this one magical setting. Heavenly.

"David, do you realize how lucky you are to have had this wonderful place in your life for so long?" Margaret Mary asked as we walked, hand in hand along the boardwalk. I didn't answer, didn't have to. My smile told her I knew and that there was no one on earth I would rather have there with me. We sat for a long time on that Animal Forest park bench listening to the calliope music from the Merry Go Round and the crack of the toy rifles from the target game. Laughing children dashed past, pursued by laughing parents. Strings of colored lights drooped from park trees, colored tubes of neon winked all around us and a late summer breeze carried the aroma of salt air, popcorn, french fries and fresh, hot doughnuts. It was one of those twinkling moments, one of those joyful instances you wished would never end. But they always do.

"You guys wanna' buy some pot?" Some sleazebag kid in a dirty t-shirt and jeans had slid onto the bench next to us. He half whispered his offer out of the side of his mouth while nervously scanning the passers-by. I turned to look at him and took my arm out from around Margaret Mary.

"Beat it." The kid looked at me. "I'm not going to say it twice. Scram."

The kid got up and scuttled away, further into the park.

"We should report him to the police," Margaret Mary said.

"Cops won't do nothin' just because we say so. Besides, he's probably selling catnip or oregano."

Margaret Mary considered me carefully. "How do you know about this sort of thing, David?" She was genuinely concerned, even worried.

"Been hearing about it down at Lefty's. Butchie, I mean Kevin, he told me a lot of that stuff is getting up here from Boston."

Margaret Mary considered this and shook her head sadly. "I wish I didn't know about that."

"Yeah, me too, but it's around," I answered.

Pot at Animal Forest Park. Total buzz kill, which was creeping in all around us. The Beatles! after almost two years of "Yeah, Yeah, Yeah" and "I Feel Fine' were singing about "I'm A Loser" and crying out for "Help!" You know change is afoot when our favorite Mop Tops are singing…

*When I was younger, so much younger than today, I never needed anybody's help in any way, But now those days are gone I'm not so self assured, And now I find I've changed my mind, I've opened up the door.*

Another popular group, The Rolling Stones, were letting us know that,

*When I'm watching my TV,*
*And a man comes on and tells me*
*How white my shirts should be,*
*But he can't be a man*
*'cause he doesn't smoke,*
*The same cigarettes as me,*
*I can't Get NO Satisfaction.*

Buzz kill was popping up everywhere. We couldn't even trust AM radio anymore.

We stood up and walked out of the park, back to my Dad's car, and took a ride out to Nubble Light. The moon was full and bright away from the lights of the town and I parked the car facing the wondrous red flare of light shining over the sea from The Nubble.

I knew a lot about Nubble Light. It was built in 1879. It was 41 feet high and could cast its light 13 miles out to sea. It had a great, booming foghorn on fog hornery days that sounded every ten seconds. A lighthouse keeper and his family lived on the Nubble, one of the last manned lighthouses in the country. But what I knew most about Nubble Light is that it was my magic place. My safe place. The serene image I kept in my mind that recalled tranquility and solace wherever I would go. The Nubble was mine in my mind. Ours, for Margaret Mary and I on this night.

Margaret Mary scooted next to me and put her head on my shoulder. We sat in silence and watched the mariner's beam brighten a path across the moonlit sea.

"David, do you realize how much our lives are going to change after this weekend?" She sighed, almost sad, yet full of wonder.

Before I could answer I got a giant lump in my throat and could not squeak out a reply. The enormity of the changes before me arrived like a freight train. I had no words.

"David, are you alright?" Margaret Mary sat up straight to look in my face. She immediately knew I wasn't.

"I'm scared too," she offered, "and excited and nervous, all at the same time. Is that how you feel?"

I started to speak, twice, and failed. I shifted in my seat, turning to look out the side window, away from Margaret Mary.

"I'm going to miss not seeing you," I finally managed to say as my eyes filled with tears.

She didn't answer right away and the silence in the car throbbed in my ears. Then Margaret Mary turned my head in her hands so I would face her.

"I am going to miss you too. Very much. I'm going to miss sitting next to you in class, walking home from school with you, doing our homework on my porch, going to Lefty's for a sandwich, just being with you."

Margaret Mary wasn't done yet but I managed to interrupt her. "Is any of this supposed to be making me feel better?"

And we laughed, sort of. Just for a moment until the reality returned.

"Will you write to me, and call me up on the weekends sometime?" I asked.

"Of course, we'll write all the time. You have a magic pen, remember?"

I do, and I did, and after a few deep breaths I felt a little better. The changes that were coming couldn't be all bad, could they? Margaret Mary leaned over and kissed me, on the cheek, then on the lips. We held each other as the magnificent red light of the Nubble swept around us as the hour grew later and the weekend passed.

We never did take that one more ride on the Wild Mouse.

*You can dance, every dance with the guy*
*Who gives you the eye, let him hold you tight,*
*You can smile, every smile for the man*
*neath the pale moonlight.*

*But don't forget who's takin' you home,*
*And in whose arms you're gonna' be,*
*So darling, save the last dance for me.*

*Oh I know, that the music's fine,*
*like sparkling wine,*
*Go and have your fun, Laugh and sing,*
*But when we're apart don't give your*
*heart to anyone.*

*Baby, don't you know I love you so?*
*Can't you feel it when we touch?*
*I will never, never let you go,*
*I love you oh so much.*

And right then I did and part of me always would.

<u>"Save The Last Dance For Me"</u> Written by Doc Pomus and Mort Shuman, recorded by The Drifters eventually reached #1 on the Billboard charts despite being released as a "B" side to "Nobody But Me" on Atlantic Reords. Dick Clark flipped the record over on American Bandstand and a classic was discovered.

# Chapter Ten

## *Boston Premiere*

**"Those of you who come here to study Law, we welcome you. Those of you who come here seeking Justice we would refer to our friends the Jesuits over at Boston University."**

This was the matriculation speech at Suffolk University on Monday, September 13, 1965. I sat in the auditorium amidst the class of being welcomed freshman. I felt like a fish, very much out of water.

**"Those of you who come here to pursue the field of journalism, and the Arts, we welcome you as well. We can teach you how to write. We can guide you as to where to look to find inspiration for your writing, however, what you write, you must decide for yourselves, with the help, if necessary, from our friends the Jesuits, just across town."**

These remarks got the required polite chuckle from our reserved, wide-eyed crowd. There would be a lot of sophisticated banter, inter-campus joking about collegiate rivalry, and urban delights, during this convivial indoctrination session. A peek into the new fellowship into which I was being welcomed.

This was my first day on campus, my exciting first day, on my own in Boston.

I had ridden the 7:10 morning commuter train from Lowell to North Station. I passed through stops in North Billerica, Wilmington, Wedgemere, and Winchester before rumbling into North Station. From there it was a short walk on Causeway Street to the edge of Beacon Hill and the Suffolk University main campus on Temple Street.

I had traced the route a week earlier with my family when we drove Margaret Mary to Logan airport for her flight to Chicago. Her father, Sean, was with us as well, and I still recall the tears in his eyes as he watched his daughter walk down the passageway to board the plane. I struggled with my own emotions as Margaret Mary paused in the airplane doorway and waved a brave goodbye to all of us. Sean was silent, inwardly reflective as we took the side trip to North Station and over to the Suffolk University campus on Temple Street. I had the route down, I promised, wishing I didn't feel so intimidated by the short journey I would be taking alone come Monday morning.

Suffolk University was founded in 1908. It was initially a private law school of around five thousand students located on the edge of the exclusive Beacon Hill section of Boston.

The school motto was;

*"Honestas et Diligentia"*

Honesty and Diligence, two qualities I hoped to enhance within myself while studying there.

The alumni of the school included several mayors of Boston, a congressman or two and lots of judges, trial lawyers and assorted local politicians. Suffolk was a good school, with a solid reputation. I secretly wondered what the hell I was doing there. I reminded myself that I was now in a class with the smart students from high schools all over the country. If they could be here, I could too. So far so good.

**"As incoming freshman we hope you will become part of our community, joining with us in continuing the proud heritage of Suffolk University. May your tenure here become a guidepost for you in life. May the knowledge you gain here be a boon not only to you but to society as well."**

With that sentiment we were dismissed. Along with the other freshman I began wandering unfamiliar hallways looking for classroom numbers, picked up course book lists and visited the bookstore and the cafeteria. In the cafeteria I found a corner table and plopped my pile of textbooks on it. I bought a cup of coffee and a cinnamon roll and checked out the room.

First thing I noticed is that I was seriously out-dressed. My standard red, green and blue checkered birthday shirt wasn't in style here. Lots of madras, which is sort of a dressed up plaid, crew neck sweaters and chinos with saddle shoes for the guys, a lot of the girls (bless their hearts) wore what looked like the bottom half of a cheerleader outfit, short skirts, knee socks, buttoned up blouses, cute little pony tails. There was a scattering of black turtlenecks, jeans and loafers on both the guys and the gals and a fledgling beard or two (on the guys).

"Anybody sitting here?" My review of the cafeteria dress code was interrupted by a jolly looking, very fat, freshman carrying a food tray that looked like it had dinner for two on board. I knew he was a freshman because in addition to the payload of chow he was lugging he had the same welcome aboard package all the new students had all been given at the morning indoctrination.

"Help yourself," I replied and the fat but friendly guy unloaded his tray onto the table. I briefly lost track of my cinnamon roll.

"My name's Jimmy Barone." Jimmy extended his hand. I shook it.

"Dave," I answered, "Dave Ferrier. Nice to meet you."

"You a freshman too huh?" He said.

I pointed at my welcome packet. "Where are you from Jimmy?"

"Farmington, that's in Connecticut, right near Hartford." Jimmy dug into cheeseburger number one, scattering French fries as he disappeared the food. It was obvious cheeseburger number two was not going to be around much longer either. I couldn't recall ever seeing anyone eat as fast.

"Miss breakfast this morning, Jimmy?" I asked, impressed.

"This is breakfast," Jimmy answered, "and lunch. Kind of a combo. I got lost on the way over here this morning, didn't have time to eat. I'm starving."

Cheeseburger number two, as I expected, was half gone. The French fries were all gone. This guy could eat.

"What do you do when you're not starving, Jimmy? What's your major?"

"Law, I guess. My father's a lawyer, wants me to be one too."

Cheeseburger number two disappeared. Jimmy slowed down a tick. He gulped down what looked like a half gallon of soda and slammed the cup down on the table.

"How about you?" He asked. "You doing law?"

"Journalism, at least for now. I might change my mind later."

"My father would kill me if I changed my mind. He said he's not paying for me to become some kind of pansy artist or something."

"Sounds like a lawyer all right. How did you like our welcoming speeches this morning?"

"All I could hear was my stomach grumbling." Jimmy laughed, "I'm glad I didn't come here looking for Justice though."

"There's always the Jesuits if you decide you need some," I offered.

"My dad doesn't like Jesuits. He's not that interested in Justice either. Like I said he's a lawyer." I think I was going to like Jimmy.

"So, you living in town?" I asked.

"Yeah, with two other guys from Farmington. One's going to Northeastern, that's Bruce, Dan's a sophomore at Berklee.

"You?" Jimmy asked.

"I live in Lowell, with my parents. I take the train in."

"Geez, I wish I could have stayed at home. My father wanted me to come here though. He graduated here in 1945, said it kept him out of the war."

Jimmy's father was starting to sound like a real piece of work.

Jimmy and I became campus buddies over the next few weeks as I fell into the routine of train ride, classes, cafeteria, more classes and another train ride.

As I got to know Jimmy better he became a guy I admired, and felt sorry for all at the same time. First off, his family was loaded. His father was Anthony Barone, big time criminal lawer with a Manhatten practice and a track record of keeping criminals, who could afford him, out of jail. Jimmy's mother, Carmen, was a ghost with a Martini in her hand who spent hours in beauty parlors and nail salons and very little time with her children.

Jimmy had a older brother, Wayne, who fled the family circle some three years back and moved to New York city to become an artist, a sculptor. He was disowned by Anthony and Carmen and missed terribly by Jimmy.

Jimmy found in food what he didn't have at home, warmth and comfort. He ate, and overate, never satisfying his hunger. After that first day he never came to a lunch room table without an extra doughnut or cinnamon roll or pastry for me. He was a generous guy with his own special interest in Rock & Roll music.

Girl groups were his thing. The Supremes, Chiffons, The Ronnettes, Orlons, Pony Tails, and just about any other group of three to five harmonizing females were Jimmy's Beatles, Elvis or Roling Stones.

When sufficiently motivated, or half in the bag, he would break out in an extremely off key chorus of "Racing in the the Street", or "Heat Wave", sometimes, "Nowhere to Run", or "You Can't Hurry Love".

What I notifced about this behavior, particularly at the weekend party he and his room-mates threw at their apartment, he always managed to get the best looking girls in the room to join him in the chorus.

Smart guy, like I said.

As I settled into a kind of foggy routine I was becoming a ghost to my family. School all day, all week, exhausted and with lots of studying to do on weekends, tired all the time.

Margaret Mary would call on weekends sometime. She talked to her father every Sunday morning and after that she would call me, but she couldn't stay on the phone long because long distance calls were expensive and she didn't want to run up her Aunt Rose's phone bill.

Teddy was working full time at the garage and I didn't see much of him either. He had a steady girl now, Carol Santos, and they spent a lot of time together.

One night while I was out driving around alone in my Dad's car a song came on the radio that I had never heard before. It was an old Hank Williams lament which had been re-recorded by a singer named B.J. Thomas. As he sang I pulled over to the side of the road to hear the song better. The words went like this…

Hear that lonesome whippoorwill
He sounds too blue to fly
The midnight train is whining low,
I'm so lonesome I could cry.

Did you ever see a night so long,
When time goes crawling by,
The moon just went behind a cloud,
To hide his face and cry.

Did you ever see a robin weep
When leaves begin to die?
Like me, he's lost the will to live,
I'm so lonesome I could cry.
The silence of a falling star,
Lights up a purple sky,
And as I wonder where you are,
I'm so lonesome I could cry.

And that is how I felt most of the time.

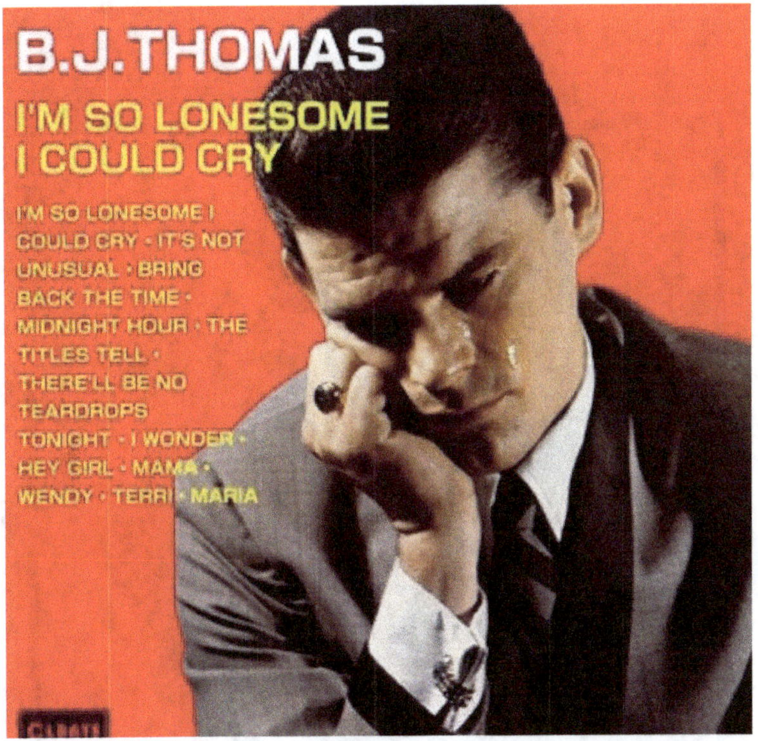


"There are happy blues, sad blues, lonesome blues, red hot blues, mad blues and loving blues. Blues is a testimony to the fullness of life."

**-Corey Harris**

<u>"I'm So Lonesome I Could Cry"</u>, Written and recorded by Hank Williams in 1949. Covered by B. J. Thomas in 1966 it reached #8 on the bIllboard charts for that year. This song was rated #111 on Rolling Stones poll of "The Greatest Hits of All Time", the only song from the 1940's to be ranked.

JAMES MONTGOMERY FLAGG
I WANT YOU
FOR U.S. ARMY
NEAREST RECRUITING STATION

# Chapter Eleven

## *Happy Birthday To Us*

On July 28, 1965 President Lyndon Johnson made the following remarks at a White House press conference. The former "peace candidate" stated that unless we radically increased our troop strength and bombing efforts in Vietnam our country would face "an Asia so threatened by communist domination that would certainly imperil the security of the United States itself."

He then set two distinct programs into motion. He raised the monthly draft quota from 17,000 young men a month to 35,000 a month. Then, as a reaction to increasing anti-war protests around the country, shepherded the Draft Card Mutilation Act through Congress which made it a major felony, punishable by five years in prison and a twenty-five thousand dollar fine to mutilate or destroy your draft card.

During our senior year in high school, in Civics class, we were reminded that as mandated by the Selective Training and Service Act, all males born in, or who were naturalized citizens of the United States, had to register for the military draft within thirty days after reaching their 18th birthday. Failure to do so was punishable by up to five years in federal prison.

This is relevant because my best buddy, Teddy Gianoulis, turned eighteen on December 8, 1965. I matched him four days later on December 12$^{th}$. On December 14$^{th,}$ Teddy and I reported to Lowell's office of the local Draft Board. A kindly woman with silver hair checked the birthdates on our driver's licenses and gave us a form to fill out and sign. When we returned them she congratulated us on doing our duty and gave us a temporary draft card. She also said we would be notified by mail as to when to report to Boston for our physical.

We must, she reminded, keep this card with us at all times. There was a poster on the wall warning us what would happen if we burned or mutilated our cards.

"Wow", Teddy proclaimed, reading his temporary card in the hallway outside the draft office. "This means we can go in the Army anytime we want."

"Or the Air Force, Navy, Marine Corps or Coast Guard," I added.

The draft card, like our driver's license and our high school diploma was yet another certificate of adulthood. Three pieces of paper that said you're not a kid anymore.

More new ground.

From what we had been hearing around town Teddy and I were just the latest in a long parade of our peers signing up for the draft. Our high school graduating class of 1965 already had several graduates enlist, among them Butchie, now Kevin, who had departed for the Navy two months ago. Our class president, Dennis Simon was in the Navy, Lester Brown in the Coast Guard. Paco Barnes from down at the gym was also in the Navy along with Antoine Davis, the lightning fast boxer Teddy and I had both sparred with in our early days at Nelson's Gym. Lots of guys chose to sign up and join up at the same time. This was an instant ticket out of Lowell for some, out of poverty for others, into the adventure for still more.

Draft board registration affected everybody in our class in some way, except the girls of course. Girls weren't eligible to get drafted. This was apparently an equality not worth fighting for. For the rest of us though it was sign up or go to jail. Teddy and I chose the sign up option.

Many newly eligible males scrambled for a wide variety of draft exemptions, the most popular and easiest to obtain being the "IIS", student deferment, technically titled, "Registrant deferred because of activity in study." In addition to the normal number of college attendees automatically granted this deferment, this educational loophole led to a nationwide rush on two year community colleges whose entrance requirements were much less stringent than four year universities. A host of private "technical" schools sprung up as well, their admission requirements generally limited to cash on hand.

For others there was the relative security of the weekends only, National Guard service, military Reserve units quickly filled up and teen marriages (supplemented by "draft babies" and deferred as "III-A", (Registrant with a child or children; or registrant deferred by reason of extreme hardship to dependents.) In the next few years this deferment, "married with children" would largely disappear as draft quotas became more difficult to fill.

Some took a more philosophical stand, like Peter Rayburn, who we learned had registered as "I-A-O", a "conscientious objector available for non-combatant military service only." Yet another path was the "IV F" classification, "Registrant not qualified for any military service." This classification excluded not only those legitimately having physical or mental handicaps, but a growing number of otherwise eligible males obtaining false medical profiles. A rash of applicants with flat feet, heart murmurs, kidney troubles and "homosexual tendencies" began showing up as impaired as possible for their draft physicals.

In all there were twenty-two different draft classifications. On this day Teddy and I were assigned to two different categories. Two buddies, friends since childhood, next door neighbors, were set apart. I had the much sought after II S student deferment, Teddy was IA, not an "if" classification, a when classification. And a seed of guilt began to grow within me.

I had taken the day off from school to come register. Teddy took a day off from the garage. The task completed I looked forward to spending the rest of the day with Teddy, something we had not had a chance to do in too long a time.

"Wanna' go down the gym, bounce around a little?" I suggested. We had both thrown our gear in the car, just in case.

"There's somebody here I want to talk to first," Teddy replied. "He's up on the second floor."

The second floor was where all the Military Recruitment offices were. And that is where Teddy wanted to go.

"C'mon in fellas," a cheerful, brush cut, immaculately uniformed United States Marine Corps Staff Sergeant intoned as we paused in the doorway of his office. He was seated behind a large wooden desk covered with brochures and leaflets touting the proud tradition of United States

Marine Corps. Teddy bounced in. I held back a moment, then followed, cautiously.

"Have a seat, fella's," the recruiter offered in his most genial tone. He indicated two wooden armchairs facing his immaculate desk. The office walls were covered with colorful posters of Marines in full dress blue uniforms standing proudly before rippling red, white and blue flags. There was a brass eagle, wings widespread, on the corner of the desk and the immediately recognizable "birdie on the ball" Marine Corps emblem everywhere else. A brass name plate centered on the desk top identified Staff Sergeant Michael Woods.

We sat. Staff Sergeant Michael Woods, we presumed, waited patiently as we settled in, still smiling. Sergeant Woods was roughly the size and shape of a refrigerator. His head was square and looked like a muscle with a crew cut. His smile seemed genuine. His eyes were sizing us up.

"I am Staff Sergeant Michael Woods. You may call me Sergeant Woods. What can I do for you guys?"

"My brother is with the Third Marine Division in Vietnam," Teddy proudly announced.

"Outstanding!" Staff Sergeant Woods replied. "That's my old outfit. How's he doing? Is he okay?"

"Says he is. I got a letter from his last week. Wanna' see it?" Teddy produced a worn and creased envelope from his pocket and extracted the red, white and blue edged letter.

"That's personal son. You should keep it between him and you. Thanks for offering though. What's your brother's name?"

"Chris", Teddy replied immediately, and then, "Lance Corporal Christopher Gianoulis. He's a machine gunner."

"0311?" Woods asked.

Teddy and I exchanged a bewildered look and shrugged our shoulders.

"Sorry," Sergeant Woods grinned. "That's Corps talk for your brother's MOS. That means Military Occupational Specialty. 0311, combat infantryman, it's what every marine is at the end of the day."

We all smiled. I didn't know why I was smiling.

"What brings you here today?" Sergeant Woods asked.

"We just signed up for our draft cards," Teddy explained. "I was thinking about maybe joining the Marines, like my brother."

Sergeant Woods clasped his hands in front of him and leaned forward across his desk.

"Let me tell you something, son. My brother is a hairdresser who likes to dress up like my mother. I, personally, am not inclined to follow his example."

This got a laugh from Teddy and I but Sergeant Woods was not joking. He stood up from behind his desk and reached for a cane leaning against the back wall. We hadn't noticed the cane before. Sergeant Woods leaned into it as he walked around to the front of his desk.

He rested against the edge of the desk and continued, "I was in Vietnam fourteen months before the Third Marines arrived in Danang. Embassy duty, Saigon. I was wounded four months ago and sent to a hospital on Okinawa, then on to San Francisco. I am now on a recuperative assignment. I volunteered for this job. You want to know why?"

We did.

I like the Vietnamese as a people. They are simple, hardworking, gracious and generally speaking, friendly bunch. And they are getting screwed. Do you guys know anything about what's going on over there?" He asked without judgment, but with little hope that we actually did.

We didn't. The Lowell Sun newspaper gave us bits and pieces sandwiched around local politics, sports, weather and what was playing in the movies. TV had grainy black and white film clips, mostly of helicopters landing in rice paddies along with fuzzy comments of reporters chanting body counts. TV had Huntley and Brinkley and somber Walter Cronkite who sounded concerned for thirty seconds and then moved on to more colorful national news.

I heard the growing debate about our involvement in the war on campus at Suffolk. Peter Rayburn, who I saw occasionally at Lefty's was on fire on the subject. He echoed the anti-war sentiment so popular on campuses across the country and as usual, backed up his opinions by quoting sources and articles I had not taken the trouble to read. So no, I didn't know much about "what was going on" over there. I realized Sergeant Woods was the first person I had actually talked to who had been there, on the ground in Vietnam, and I figured I could learn a lot by listening to what he had to say.

"My brother Chris says we're winning but a lot of his friends are getting killed," Teddy offered.

"That's true son, we can win over there but we are going to have to send a lot more Marines over there to do it. The Viet Cong are slaughtering hundreds of civilians, men, women and children, every day. Our country has pledged to protect these people from the communists. And that is where the Marines come in."

"Why can't the South Vietnam Army guys fight the VC guys?" Teddy asked. By this point in the conversation I realized I was going to learn a lot more by listening than by talking. I was listening very closely.

Sergeant Woods shifted his weight on the desk and continued, "They are poorly trained, poorly led and poorly motivated," He answered. "If we don't back them up they will lose. You want to know why?"

Teddy and I nodded, no words necessary. Sergeant Woods wasn't preaching, he was explaining, patiently, as best he knew how what he believed and why he believed it.

"Doesn't fucking matter," he growled as he walked back around the desk to his chair. When he was seated he continued, "Why" is politics. Marines don't give a damn about politics. Marines do give a damn about doing the right thing. I believe helping the people of South Vietnam fight the invaders from the North is the right thing and as soon as my leg is better I'm going back over there to do just that."

Sergeant Woods spoke in a calm, measured tone that rang, clearly, of sincerity and of a concept not in high favor at the time, at least not among the younger generation, Teddy and my generation; patriotism.

My father was a patriot. He served honorably in World War II. Both my uncles, Dick and Artie, had also served. My grandfather served with the 26th, "Yankee" Division in France in WWI and that was as deep into my family history as I knew. There was a bond there, a membership in the fraternity of veterans who served their country in time of war. I was drawn to this fraternity and always assumed I would one day follow their footsteps into the military. It was part of the rite of passage, a family tradition, duty owed for privilege granted.

Teddy and I sat spellbound. No one had ever spoken to us in this manner about the war before. The newspapers and the TV reported and printed a lot of political pro and con "why's". There wasn't much talk about the "right thing".

"Do either of you know what happened in the la Drang Valley about three weeks ago?" He asked, not expecting us to have a clue. Which we didn't.

Sergeant Woods pulled a sheaf of papers from his desk drawer. Arranging them neatly on the desk top he said, "This is an after-action report. Probably classified, I got it from a friend in the Pentagon who keeps me up to date on what's going on in Vietnam."

Sergeant Woods held the paper up. "On November 14th, last month, elements of the United States 7th Cavalry engaged an NVA regiment in a three day battle in which 237 American soldiers were killed, another three hundred or so wounded. Approximately twelve hundred enemy soldiers were killed. ARVN units, that means South Vietnamese troops, lost close to a thousand killed or wounded. Do you know why the ARVN troops lost twice as many soldiers as we did?"

We didn't.

"They are poorly trained, poorly led and poorly motivated. All three of which you will not be as United States Marines. This war in Vietnam is likely to last a long time. The Viet Cong and the North Vietnamese Army are a tough, vicious enemy. If you end up going to Vietnam, and it's likely you will, you want to go with the best training and with the best fighters you can. There is no better fighting force on the planet than the Marine Corps. That is who you want to go into combat with, for your own good."

Teddy and I squirmed in our seats. The silence in the room was very loud. Finally, Sergeant Woods spoke, in a very soft voice, "So you two just got your draft cards today and are waiting to take your physical, right?"

We nodded. He continued. "Odds are you are both going into the service, sooner or later. You both 1A?"

Teddy nodded as I blurted out, "I am in school, Suffolk University in Boston."

"So you're "2S". Are you going to stay in school?"

Despite my misgivings, I answered yes, at least for now.

Sergeant Woods now looked much more professionally interested in the two of us. He centered a yellow pad of paper on his desk, took out a pen.

"What's your full name Ted?"

"Teddy, I mean. Theodorus, that's Greek for Theodore, but everybody calls me Teddy, Teddy Gianoulis." Sergeant Woods began writing.

"How about you, Dave? Full name." The pen was poised.

"Ferrier, David Owen. I answered automatically.

Sergeant Woods jotted this down and turned his attention back to Teddy.

"When were you thinking of joining up, Ted? We can start the paperwork today."

Teddy squirmed a little in his seat.  The wheel was turning fast.

"I haven't talked about this with my Dad or my sister yet. They don't know I want to enlist or anything."

"That's no problem, Ted. I'm sure you don't want to leave until after the holidays, so you can spend them with your family. We can arrange it so you don't actually leave until after the first of next year."

Teddy seemed to feel better about that. He gave me a "what do you think?" look. This was one decision I didn't want to be any part of. I did hope he would take a little more time to think about this though.

"Maybe you should talk to your Dad and Connie before you make up your mind," I offered.

Sergeant Woods looked like he was going to hit me with the desk.

"Dave's right, Ted. You should talk this over with your family," He crooned. "But we can get you started with a physical. You're going to need to get one anyway. Both of you are, for your draft classification. This way you can pick the date you want to go down to Boston and be examined and we'll have the paperwork all ready when you decide when you want to leave for boot camp."

The wheel, still turning. Sergeant Woods was pushing some papers across the desk for Teddy to sign. Just Teddy, I hoped.

"When I join can I get to be a machine gunner like Chris?" Teddy asked.

"When you enlist in the Marine Corps you get to choose the MOS you want. We will make machine gunner your first choice."

I noticed he had not answered the question.

"When you sign up for the Marine Corps how many years do you go in for?" I asked as pleasantly as possible.

"Four years," He replied cheerfully, "And I can guarantee they will be the best four years of your life." Sergeant Woods appeared very confident about how happy the rest of our lives were going to be.

"Dave," he continued, "I can arrange it so you and Teddy can go in on the "Buddy" system, that means you will leave on the same day and go to boot camp together. Lots of guys like going in with a buddy."

"What about after boot camp?" I asked.

"That will depend on what training you choose. Remember you get to pick your job when you join the Corps. If you pick different jobs you will likely go to different places to be trained. So what do you say, Dave? You want to get your physical out of the way the same day as Teddy?"

More papers slid across the desk. This time toward me.

"Uh," I stalled, "I think I'm going to wait a while before I sign up for a physical. I've got finals next week and a lot of studying to do. I think I'm going to wait," I replied, hoping Teddy would do the same.

"How about you, Ted. Next Thursday all right?"

Teddy nodded and signed the papers. Sergeant Woods pulled them back and offered Teddy a handshake. He gave Teddy a packet with carbon copies of the papers he signed and a round trip train ticket to Boston, a bus pass from North Station to South Station and two meal passes for the Boston Naval Shipyard Induction Center. He explained the logistics to Teddy and said, "You've made a wise decision Ted. I'll have your physical results back in about two weeks, then come see me and we'll pick a date for you to start boot camp."

"Does this mean I'm in the Marines now?" Teddy seemed a little bewildered by the pace of events. So was I.

"Not quite yet, Ted. You have to pass the physical first, but I'm sure you will. Dave, you sure you don't want to get your physical with Teddy?"

"Can't, finals," I replied, relieved.

"Okay then." Sergeant Woods stood up behind his desk, dismissing us. "See you in a couple of weeks, Ted. Dave, if you change your mind, just call me here, or come by."

I nodded, we left. Back on the street I asked Teddy, "Are you sure about this?"

"I think so," Teddy replied. "I'm gonna' tell my Dad and Connie tonight. I think my Dad might get kinda' mad."

"What about Chris? Don't you think you should find out what he thinks before you do anything final?"

"You think I should tell him?"

"Definitely, you should write to him and not sign anything else until you hear back." This was advice aimed at buying my buddy a little more time.

"Yeah, you're right," Teddy admitted. "But I'm still going to get the physical. Maybe we can ride in on the train together."

"And ride home together," I added. I was not ready to lose Teddy just yet.

Teddy took his physical the following Thursday. We rode into Boston on the morning train together but parted ways as he took the bus over to South Station and the Boston Naval Yard.

That evening Teddy and I rode home on separate trains. His physical ended mid-afternoon and I had a late class. As I rode home that night I was thinking alot about Staff Sergeant Michael Woods. He was, beyond question or doubt, a patriot. He had devoted his life to serving his country and believed to his soul in the principles of right and wrong and how our country was obligated to embody the "right thing to do".

This was not a popular position right now. Anti-war, anti-draft sentiment was sweeping the country, dividing the nation. I had not really thought much about this until the nice, silver haired lady handed me my draft card. Now it was personal and I would have to make a decision.

Teddy had already stepped forward. Butchie, now Kevin, along with several others from the gym and my high school class were already in the military. Others, such as Peter Rayburn, were passionately questioning the war, and I realized this too could be a way to be a patriot.

I remembered the last thing Sergeant Woods said before Teddy and I left his office. He walked us to the door and said, "You two have a decision to make. You can do the right thing, the wrong thing, or nothing at all. I'm not going to try and tell you which is which but you will have to live with your decision for the rest of your life. So, think it over carefully."

We said goodbye in the hallway and tonight, on the train home all I could think of was that this "rest of your life" business was getting more immediate all the time. I hoped I would choose the right thing.

*I got nowhere to run baby, nowhere to hide,*

*It's not love I'm running from,*

*Just the heartbreak I know will come.*

*'Cause I know you're no good for me,*
*But you've become a part of me,*
*Everywhere I go your face I see,*
*Every step I take you take with me,*
*Nowhere to run baby, nowhere to hide.*

<u>"Nowhere To Run"</u> Written by Brian Holland, Lamont Dozier and Eddie Holland. Recorded by Martha & The Vandellas in 1965 when it rose to # 8 on the Billboard charts.

# Chapter Twelve

## *Fadda' Who?*

"You need to be sitting down when I tell you this."

Is how I started when I got to Margaret Mary's house that afternoon.

Margaret Mary crossed immediately to her favorite front porch seat and folded her hands in her lap as she always did when we started these discussions. She waited patiently for me to seat myself. I settled in, took a deep breath and announced,

"Peter Rayburn is going to be a priest!"

Margaret Mary blinked, twice, and before she could say anything. I rushed on.

"I was just talking to him down at Lefty's and he says he's going to leave Boston University after this semester and enter the novitiate in Newburgh, New York in the fall. He's already signed up for it and everything!"

That was it, my rush of words was used up. I squirmed in my chair and waited for Margaret Mary to comment.

"That is wonderful," she began, "Did he tell you why he has decided to do this?"

"He did, wanna' know what he said?" The look of patient tolerance on Margaret Mary's face was a wonder to behold. I rushed on, "You know how Peter always asks "Why?"

Margaret Mary nodded with more patient tolerance.

"He said that he now believes. 'Why?' is the wrong question. He said nobody actually knows the reason why about anything. They're just guessing or giving their own opinion. He finally decided that what he should be asking is 'Who?'"

"Who?" Margaret Mary repeated.

"Yeah," I answered, nodding my head as fast as I could. "He said that everything has to come from somewhere, right? Well, something or somebody had to start everything off, right? Peter has decided that the only person or thing that could be is God and he's gonna' be a priest to learn more about God."

Somehow this babble of words made sense to me. Margaret Mary was my "who", to help me understand "why".

Smiling her delightful smile she sat back in her chair. Then she said, "Isn't it wonderful, David?"

"What? That Peter's gonna' be a priest?"

"No, that Peter has found out who he wants to be and that he is going to become that person. Just like you and I will one day."

Margaret Mary had come home for Christmas only two days ago. My father let me drive into Boston, to the airport, alone, for the first time. Teddy had volunteered to come with me. Sean, of course, was going to leave work early and come along. I talked them both out of it. I wanted, very much, to have this time alone with her before we were swallowed up by the families and the festivities and all the holiday details

There were lots of confusing freeway exchanges, tunnels, a toll booth, congested traffic and airport confusion to be negotiated, but all of the tension of the drive was worth it when I saw Margaret Mary emerge from the terminal, suitcase in hand, searching for me. My heart did the "skip a beat" thing when I saw her. I waved, she ran toward me, I lifted her clean of the ground when I hugged her. She was all smiles as I put her down and she looked around.

"Are you alone?" There was a hint of disappointment in her voice.

"I am," I answered. "Your father wanted to come, so did Teddy, but I talked them out of it. I just wanted to have some time, just us."

We hugged again, harder, then started off for the car. On the way back to Lowell Margaret Mary told me all about her school in Chicago. She had aced all her courses, of course, was on the school student activities council and was volunteering at a food bank in downtown Chicago. Her Aunt Rose was teaching her all the steps to Irish folk dancing called "Ceili" and she was going to perform with a dance group in March.

She asked about Suffolk and how I liked Boston. I told her I was learning the ropes, passing all my courses and riding the train back and forth to Lowell every day. I told her about Teddy and the Marine Corps and how we both had to sign up for the draft. I told her Butchie, now Kevin, was in the Navy and that Sean seemed to be doing very well and couldn't wait to see her. We chatted, laughed, reminisced and sat very close together all the way home.

In all too short a time we were in front of her house. The porch door swung open and Sean rushed out, all smiles for his daughter. They hugged and helloed and I pulled away, leaving them to their reunion. It felt a lot more like Christmas than before Margaret Mary's plane had landed.

When I had spoken to Peter Rayburn earlier in the day and received the news about his becoming a priest we had also discussed our experiences in signing up for the draft. Peter's birthday was around Thanksgiving and he had already been down to the draft board when Teddy and I signed up.

"I asked to be classified as a conscientious objector," Peter stated, looking me dead in the eye. "If I have to go in the Army I will, but I don't think I could kill anybody."

Which I had never really given any serious thought to. With the draft, just like everything else I was just doing these days I did what I was told or what I figured people wanted me to be doing. I was marking time in college because I had no idea of what I actually wanted to do. I was enjoying going into Boston every day, riding subways, hanging around in coffee shops and playing poker in the Suffolk University Student Union cafeteria between classes, sometimes during classes.

I listened with interest to my fellow students, who seemed a lot more confident about who they were and what they were going to be, but I heard a lot more bravado, which is a nice word for bullshit, than blueprint.

Despite all the promises, college, up till now, for me, was still mostly learn, memorize, repeat. My journalism classes were mostly author worship with mandates to imitate their style and punctuate properly. Good grammar and correctly placed commas were far more important than fresh ideas. At least so far.

I was drifting and I knew it. Now Peter had not only found his path, but his courage as well. If I didn't figure out something soon I was going to be left behind, a grown up child. I sure didn't want that. I could hardly wait to talk this subject over with Margaret Mary now that she was home.

"Peter said he's goin' to the rectory tonight to see Father Murphy to talk to him about becoming a priest. He wanted to know if we would meet him afterwards because he wanted to know what you thought about it."

"He said that? That he wanted to know what I thought?" Margaret Mary seemed pleased.

"Yup, he said maybe we could meet at the Pewter Pot about nine o'clock. I can pick you up and we can drive over."

"David, we can walk to the Pewter Pot, it's not that far."

"If God wanted us to walk he would never have let me get my driver's license. You can ask Peter, he's gonna' be a priest."

Which got a smile and more patient tolerance from Margaret Mary.

The Pewter Pot was the more genteel version of Lefty's, a tea and muffin shop that served polite sandwiches and homemade soup. It was where we went on a date after a movie or a dance. The muffins were pretty good but the sandwiches were smaller than the ones at Lefty's.

Peter was there when Margaret Mary and I arrived. He was seated at a corner table. He was wearing his beret. He stood up when we got to the table and pulled out a chair for Margaret Mary. When we were all seated he said, "Thanks for coming." And directly to Margaret Mary, "Did Dave tell you about what I've decided to do?"

"Yes, and I think it is wonderful. When did you know?" Margaret Mary could hardly contain her excitement, her genuine interest in how Peter had arrived at his decision.

"It wasn't any one thing," Peter replied. "It was a lot of little things that just seemed to add up."

"Like what?" It was my turn to hardly contain myself. This was stuff I needed to know, wanted to know.

"All the facts and theories, formulas and explanations, all the information we've been taught in school always seemed incomplete to me," Peter began in earnest, burning to make his point. "Our education is supposed to be preparing us for life, right?"

Peter wasn't asking, he was telling. "All I feel like I'm being prepared for is to memorize facts and follow rules which don't always make sense. The harder I look for the truth the more I find nobody really knows what the truth is."

Peter was sounding a lot like the way I had been thinking. The more I learned the less I believed. And I kept thinking about everything we've been taught about religion, about

God. Maybe faith was more important than knowledge. Maybe God was the right person to ask.

"What did Father Murphy say when you told him?" Margaret Mary asked.

"He told me this is a big decision and I should think it through carefully. He said a call to the priesthood can be very strong for some and a false path for others. My feeling is very strong."

"I know you are going to be a wonderful priest," Margaret Mary offered.

The waitress came over and we ordered a pot of tea and a blueberry muffin. Margaret Mary and I always split the blueberry muffin. I ate the top, she ate the bottom. I considered this karma.

"Have you told your parents yet? What did they say when you told them you weren't going to finish law school?" Margaret Mary asked.

"They want me to take it slow and think it through as well. My Dad really wanted me to become a lawyer, but I am going to Newburgh Seminary this fall. I've made up my mind."

"Well, I think it's a wonderful idea," Margaret Mary answered as our tea and muffin arrived.

"How about you Mags?" Peter had adopted Margaret Mary's recent nickname. "What are your plans after college?"

I leaned forward in my chair. This was a subject Margaret Mary and I had only discussed in passing. Up to now it had always seemed too much, too soon. I'd think about it tomorrow, or the next day.

Margaret Mary took a sip of her tea and replied, "I thought about going into teaching, like my father, but that is starting to feel like something I'm supposed to do. I'm waiting to find out what I really want to do."

"Well, you have plenty of time," Peter replied. "By the time you're a senior I'm positive you will have a plan all worked out."

Margaret Mary beamed, Peter's opinion was important to her.

"How about you Dave? Not planning on making Lefty's a career are you?" Peter smiled as he asked, for which I felt grateful, though still dumbfounded.

"David will be a famous writer. I just know it," Margaret Mary announced. "He had a story printed in the Phoenix newspaper in Boston! It was about being a freshman student in Boston. It was funny and really true."

"I saw it," Peter replied. "Really well done. My friends liked it too. "Innocents Abroad", right?"

I grinned, happily.

"I don't understand," Margaret Mary said, "What does Innocents Abroad have to do with David's story?"

'Stole it," Peter said, grinning. "From Mark Twain, lock, stock and barrel. Am I right?"

"Adapted," I replied. "Us writers like to think we adapted the story." And suddenly I was flush with the pleasure and the realization that this was the very first time I had ever referred to myself as a writer. Margaret Mary, aware as ever, reached over and squeezed my hand. She knew it too.

"Let's make a pact," Margaret Mary suggested, "Let's all be exactly what we want to be and if anyone tries to talk us out of it we will meet right here and talk ourselves back into it."

She put her hand on the table top, palm up. I put my hand in hers. Peter put his hand in mine.

"Deal," I said.

"I'm in," Peter added.

And so we three chatted on, secure in our assumptions, knowing without realizing we had all set forth on an unknown path that would carry us beyond childhood, to wherever that may be.

(Reprinted from the Cambridge Phoenix Weekly Free Newspaper 10/24/65):

## The Innocents Aboard
## Or
## The New Freshman's Progress

For months following my acceptance into the freshman class at Suffolk University in the Fall of 1965 I had contemplated the illustrious and magical journey I would be embarking upon during my expedition into the great and wonderful City of Boston.

For this journal I shall endeavor to describe my travels not through the jaded and city-wise eyes of the daily commuter, nor of the entrenched native, cozily apartmented and dormitoried throughout the city. Rather I would chronicle my journeys through the eyes of an innocent, which I certainly was, and a correspondent, which I certainly hoped to become.

Before setting out on my pilgrimage of discovery I had to secure a reliable form of transportation, one which could convey me through the myriad of streets, avenues, boulevards, causeways, alleys and footpaths I would be traversing. Taxi cabs were far beyond my financial means, buses too lumbering and hamstrung by perpetually clogged traffic. Afoot was well, too pedestrian. Which left the most mysterious and cosmopolitan form of conveyance known to man, and only urbanite man at that, the subterranean city-wide, subway system.

But where to begin? How to board? And even more important how to debark once boarded, and return to where one began? Too much thought on this would surely have discouraged me altogether so I decided to begin at the beginning and descend into the Portal at the Park Street station.

Upon my arrival in the underworld I was required to exchange my coinage for the quaint and copper discs of the local economy. Appropriate tokens in hand I turned the turnstile and stepped for the very first time onto the semi-grand concourse beneath Boston's famous Common.

The trick here fellow traveler is not to look at all like it is your first time on the bustling platform. One is best served by standing nonchalantly, never pacing or gazing longingly into the darkened and mysterious tunnels. This I soon mastered and set about to observing my fellow passengers. Most wore some sort of overcoat, car coat, jacket or sweater (it was full autumn). Some toted shopping bags, others clutched briefcases, book bags or purses, large and small. Only the uninitiated gazed into the tunnels until there was, at first, a faint rumbling, then a dim beam of light in the distance followed in quick order by the sudden appearance of a lumbering, spark belching, squealing, squeaking orange and white cable car filled to the windows with standing, sitting and scrunched together passengers.

The beast would roll to a stop, rubbery doors would slide open. Some got out, some got on. In a haste I scrambled aboard. My adventure had begun.

Grabbing a strap, the seats were all taken, we jerked forward a few times and then rolled and squealed out of the station. Boylston, Arlington, Copley Square and Kenmore stations passed by until an intriguing destination christened BU Central caught my eye. I debarked, shoulder to shoulder with fellow travelers and ascended into the daylight once more.

BU, I well knew, was Boston University where my hometown amigo, Peter Rayburn presently matriculated. I decided I must view his surroundings and found myself engulfed by Academia. Stately brick buildings, high windowed and multi-floored, edged the wide sidewalks and well tended lawns. The pathways were patrolled by earnest herds of students, be-scarfed, and jacketed in variations of red and black, the school colors, I presumed. As I strolled about the campus and surrounding area I found myself in much the same atmosphere as the one I had so recently left behind, many stations ago at Suffolk University. There were coffee shops, bookstores, clothiers, even a florist proclaiming their loyalty to good old BU. The more I looked around the more it looked the same. I do not believe that in my entire reconnoitering I encountered a single native over the age of twenty one, rosy cheeked, neatly coiffed and almost entirely Caucasian.

Satisfied I had sufficiently explored the area I descended once again into the depths and boarded yet another train I sincerely hoped was not traveling in the direction I had just come. I passed exotic sounding stations named Packard's Corner, Harvard Avenue, which I knew from pre-planning had nothing to do with Harvard University, Washington Street, Chestnut Hill and finally, at the end of the line, South Street and, of all things, Boston College.

Why there must be in the same city, indeed even the same vicinity, a Boston College and a Boston University confounded me as I could not imagine the difference. Nevertheless I disembarked figuring the similarity must in some way be attributable to the Jesuits.

Emerging once again into the daylight I found myself in yet another sea of students. This tribe however dressed in various combinations of maroon and gold. There were also lots of embroidered eagles about. Otherwise it was more of the same, youth in bloom, good haircuts, lots of Caucasians. I tried to cover my disappointment at the sameness of it all and endeavored to find the subtle differences, without success. After a brief reconnoiter I returned to the underworld and set sail for home, or Park Street station which came first.

This concluded the first stage of my journey through Boston and its Burroughs. My subsequent sojourns would take me to wild and exotic places like the Italiano flavored North End, the Harps and Shamrock infested South End, to the enticing entertainments of The Combat Zone, also politely called the Theatre District, and across the River Charles to Kendall Square, Harvard Yard and Lechmere Park.

If I could manage the tokens.

Note: I promised the Phoenix two more articles such as this which they enthusiastically agreed to publish. I never delivered. I was doing more and more of that lately.

JINGLE BELL JUKEBOX
~ AN EARLY ROCK-N-ROLL CHRISTMAS ~
12 TIMELESS HOLIDAY FAVORITES FEATURING
ELVIS PRESLEY WITH THE JORDANAIRES · BRENDA LEE ·
BOBBY HELMS WITH THE ANITA KERR SINGERS · THE BEACH BOYS · CHUCK BERRY
JAN & DEAN · ANDY WILLIAMS · THE EVERLY BROTHERS & THE BOYS TOWN CHOIR
ROY ORBISON · CHARLES BROWN · PERRY COMO WITH MITCHELL AYRES & HIS ORCHESTRA
& THE RAY CHARLES SINGERS · GENE AUTRY WITH CARL COTNER'S ORCHESTRA

# Chapter Thirteen

## *Santa Claus Is Back In Town*

The Christmas season officially arrived in my world every year the first time I heard Bobby Helms sing "Jingle Bell Rock" on any AM radio station, any day after Thanksgiving. The tune, as if you didn't know, begins like this…

*Jingle Bell, Jingle Bell, Jingle Bell Rock,*
*Jingle Bells swing and jingle bells ring,*
*Snowin' and blowin' up bushels of fun,*
*Now the jingle hop has begun.*

*Jingle bell, Jingle Bell, Jingle Bell rock,*
*Jingle Bells chime in Jingle Bell time,*
*Dancin' and Prancin' in Jingle Bell Square,*
*In the frosty air.*

And so on.

The lyrics may fade in and out but the melody, the tune, is guaranteed to remain in your head until at least New Year's Eve. The rest of the holiday season soundtrack included

Brenda Lee, "Rockin' Around The Christmas Tree," Gene Autry crooning "Rudolph The Red Nosed Reindeer" and Elvis having a "Blue Christmas." And no Christmas medley is ever complete without Nat King Cole singing…

*Chestnuts roasting on an open fire,*
*Jack Frost nipping at your nose…*

And so on.

This was, and is, Magical Holiday Music with a thirty day, end of year life span that, thankfully resurfaces every twelve months. Occasionally a new tune would drop into the mix. The Beach Boys gave us "Little Saint Nick," Eartha Kitt sighed, "Santa Baby" and Dion DiMucci added "Please Come Home For Christmas." Kids giggled without comprehension at "I Saw Mommy Kissing Santa Claus" and the Chipmunks, Alvin, Simon and Theodore chirped The Christmas Song (Christmas Don't Be Late). The list went on, goes on, sounding better and more diverse each year.

In addition to the caroling, new and old, Christmas time in Lowell meant lots of colored lights round shop windows and street lamps, festive wreaths fashioned from pine, balsam and eucalyptus on welcoming doors, plastic reindeer and cardboard sleighs in yards and on rooftops with lots of semi-Santas scattered around town. People on the downtown sidewalks seemed a little friendlier, the snow itself a little whiter, the air fresh and crisp with just the right amount of chill. Traffic lights of red and green never looked more appropriate, fruitcakes in a can never tasted better and the world, for just that little while, seemed to stop arguing, debating, disagreeing and growing worse.

There was a very special, once a year anticipation, just before dawn, in the first moments of waking up, of the knowledge that nearby was a room brightened by a shimmering Christmas tree beneath which were gaily wrapped presents. Presents to be received, presents to be presented, gifts to be shared and blessings for all. The childhood joys of getting gifts had been enhanced, multiplied many times over by the rewards of giving gifts. I shared in the delight of my family as they opened gifts, however modest, that I had chosen and purchased for them and we had purchased for each other.

On Christmas morning, one noise, however slight, would generally rouse the three of us, my brothers and I, to visit our magical living room with all its treasures. After plugging in the percolating kitchen coffee pot we would tap, delicately on our parent's bedroom door signaling our readiness to start the unwrapping of the gifts and the joy of the season.

So it was in the early morning hours of Christmas proper, December 25, 1965, that my brother, John, tore into the colorfully wrapped bundle tagged with his name that he snatched from beneath our family Christmas tree. There was no taking turns here, it was survival of the fittest on Christmas morning around the tree. Once we had all woken up, sipped coffee and gathered in the living room the opening and exchange of presents began at a rapid and joyful pace.

Outside our living room window a silvery Christmas morning emerged from the darkness as we gathered in the living room. Having any form of daylight brighten our gift opening ritual was a new circumstance, all past assaults on our presents had taken place long before sunrise as the sleepless children that we were roused the household to start the festivities hours before the rising of the sun.

This year however there was sleeping in, sort of, as a new tradition of attending Midnight Mass at our local church. This new Christmas Eve/Christmas Morning worship ritual kept us out and about till the early morning hours. On this very special Eve the Immaculate Conception church held a Christmas High Mass, (the long one), at midnight. The church would be alight with glorious gatherings of tall candles, countless bouquets of bright red and white poinsettias, the altar would contain a life sized manger with Baby Jesus, Joseph and Mary, artificial sheep, a plastic cow, three elegant kings and a bright star above a full size wooden manger. A heavenly choir sang, with a mighty organ resonating in accompaniment. Incense filled the air as families with sleepy children filled the pews.

Following the church service there was a nocturnal gathering at our kitchen table with fresh cinnamon rolls and hot chocolate. By tradition we could open one present each before bed time, the rest had to wait till the not far off morning. My mother would present the presents, modest in scale to the treasures that awaited. We would open packages most often containing peppermint candy canes, tubes of red and green jelly beans, fancy hand soap and Old Spice After Shave. Yawning would then commence and we would retire, however briefly, for the night.

Come morning our Christmas tree twinkled and sparkled in the corner of the room and beneath it wonderful piles and heaps of presents cloaked in wrapping paper awaited us all. As John got his first look at his official Ted Williams Salt Water fishing rod and reel, Bob tore into the bundle containing a new guitar strap and carry case for his much prized Gibson electric guitar. Not to be denied I was admiring my new Benrus Sportsman model wristwatch in its leather (ette) case.

Mom and Dad sat patiently nearby as their almost grown children rummaged through the pile. In due time Mom received her annual bottle of White Shoulders perfume, from me, a cat and mouse embroidered set of hand towels from Bob and two handmade (by him) pot holders from John. Dad prospered as well, fur lined gloves for the winter cold, an Old Spice Bath and Body collection and a set of Handyman screwdrivers, four in all, of varying shapes and sizes.

This year, in addition to her favorite perfume, I bought my mother a cameo pin she had admired in a magazine. For my father a leather key ring and wallet and for each of my brothers an official Boston Bruins black and gold hooded sweatshirt. I also had gifts for Margaret Mary, Sean and Teddy which I would deliver later in the day.

There were more gifts of course, an assortment of sweaters, scarfs and knitted caps nestled among hockey sticks, a Revell plastic model kit of a B-24 Bomber, the kind my father flew in World War II, the Ventures Christmas album (for my guitar playing brother, Bob), a General Electric Deluxe Electric skillet with "Double Non-Stick Coating" for my Mom and the big one, the "family present" set up in our newly finished basement.

"Down cellar" was a brand new, Sears & Roebuck, 7 foot, green felt pool table with "smooth as slate" honeycomb bed, four one piece, forty two inch pool cues, sixteen shiny new billiard balls with wooden rack and several cubes of blue cue chalk completing the package. The pool table was our big gift, a family present, to be shared equally by my brothers and myself. It would provide hours of enjoyment, games of chance and skill and become a gathering place for friends and family.

From the kitchen the delicious aroma of an overnight cooked turkey filled the air. While it would be hours before we sat down to our Christmas meal, a platter of apple cider doughnuts waited on the sideboard to hold us over until our midday feast. Sated as we were with gift unwrapping and swapping, as we contentedly munched doughnuts and shared smiles I became keenly aware once again of the sanctity of our family. Santa Claus was not responsible for our joy, Baby Jesus, despite the prominent presence of our vintage Nativity scene, was not responsible, it was just us, the Ferrier family intact and safe and secure in each others company. Just for now, at least for this one day, the trials and troubles, forebodings and fears of the past year evaporated, we were as one, as all families should be.

At the end of the day yet another Christmas song danced into my head, softly, the lyrics a promise and a prayer. It goes like this:

*Have yourself a merry little Christmas*
*Let your heart be light,*
*From now on your troubles will be*
*out of sight.*

*Have yourself a merry little Christmas
Make the yuletide gay,
From now on your troubles will be far away.*

*Here we are as in olden days
Happy golden days of yore,
Faithful friends who are dear to us
Gather near to us once more.*

*Through the years we all will be together
If the fates allow,
Hang a shining star upon the highest bow.*

*And have yourself a merry little
Christmas now.*

And this one last time, we did.


<u>"The Christmas Song"</u>, Written by Mel Torme and Bob Wells, Recorded by Nat King Cole in 1946. It has been re-released every year since.

# Chapter Fourteen

## *I'm Happy Just To Dance With You*

## *(Almost)*

I was more than a little drunk as I held up a wall at Jimmy's Friday night, Marlborough Street, hootenanny style, BYOB apartment party in Boston. I was staying in town for the weekend, sleeping over at Jimmy's as I had come to do over the past few weeks.

The deal was I'd bring Jimmy's roommates, Pat Dacy and Ron Bukowski, a case of beer and I'd sleep on the living room sofa. The thing was after they got the case of beer they'd sleep under the sofa and I'd pass out somewhere in the general vicinity. Jimmy was usually the only one of us who actually slept in a bed on weekends.

This being drunk thing was kind of new to me. I had chugged a few beers up in Lowell, drank in the ID "liberal' bars where everybody knew your name, but never really allowed myself to get as wasted as some of my buddies. I had slowly watched several guys I knew from Shedd Park and high school become weekend, then weekday drunks, sloppy, belligerent, high maintenance and trouble. I didn't find it attractive or fun.

Then I went to Boston and learned to sip economical wine poured from stubby green bottles stoppered by corks at college parties. I liked the wine and let it sneak up on me and throw a fuzzy blanket over my brain. I still knew when to draw the line, mostly, but I found the line was moving further into the bottle every time. Nevertheless, I sipped the Rose', or the Chablis, regretted the Spanada and Boone's Farm, and lied to myself about maintaining a reasonable sense of equilibrium. Wine seemed more the way sophisticated people got shit-faced.

Meanwhile the room around me was packed with drinking, smoking, dancing, laughing, sweating, college students who were making out, getting drunk, and discussing the great social issues of the day while trying not to fall over. I was seriously trying not to throw up.

I was a couple of weeks into my second semester at Suffolk. Semester one had been a "getting to know you" type situation, finding my way around the campus and the city, making acquaintances, scheduling classes, drifting farther away from my home. Glenmere Street was now just a place I went to sleep and eat after school, after long train rides, after noisy parties like this one.

I had become pretty good friends with Jimmy Barone by this time. I liked him, he was a smart guy, had a good sense of humor, a tremendous appetite and a really cool apartment right near the campus. I had become unofficial weekend roommate number four. My rent was a case of Carling Black Label Beer. College at this point was only so-so, but I was really enjoying the big city night life.

"Hey! You're not dancing!" A girl in a black turtleneck sweater, blue jeans and boots proclaimed as she bobbed and weaved in front of me.

"I'm dancing on the inside," I answered, trying to focus on the outside.

"Well, come on," she grabbed my hand and started pulling me into the center of the room. "Dance with me, on the inside."

I stumbled after her onto the patch of Indian carpet serving as the dance floor. Loud music from a band I did not recognize played over the din of conversations. Black turtleneck girl spun to face me and started gyrating around. I did the same. The room was gyrating around too. Life was good.

We did this for two more songs until silence descended on the room and a new record was placed on the turntable. Joan Baez began to warble. The dancing stopped.

"I didn't get your name," I said as we walked hand in hand off the dance floor. Black turtleneck girl didn't answer as she led me to a quiet corner, with couch, that we both flopped onto.

"Rebecca," she answered, wiggling next to me on the couch. "But I like "Becca", never Becky." Becca moved again. This time she moved onto my lap. Fast, very fast. I stopped thinking about throwing up, started thinking about my lap.

"Becca' smelled of patchouli, a very "collegie" smell I first smelled in Boston. Her hair was cut short, not like a guy, but very cute. She bulged in all the right places under the black turtleneck sweater and filled out her blue jeans without a wrinkle. She put one arm around my shoulders and looked me in the eye. She had great eyes.

"I'm guessing you have a name too. Wanna' tell me?" Her smile wasn't bad either. Really not bad at all.

"OK, Becca. I'm Dave." I was running out of snappy answers, but the room was spinning less and I was getting very focused on this girl who was now sitting on my lap, smiling. Strange things happen in this world.

We made tiny, small talk as Joan Baez warbled on. Northeastern for her.  History major. From Connecticut. First year in Boston. Didn't know whose apartment this was. Came with her friends, Judy and somebody. She didn't bother to point them out.

She thought journalism was a cool major. Asked what kind of writer I wanted to be and before I could lie about an answer she leaned in and kissed me. Hard. With tongue. I wasn't feeling drunk anymore but the room seemed a lot warmer. I kissed her back, more tongues. More squirming. When we finally came up for air Becca asked, "Wanna' walk me home?"

Standing up was going to be a little painful, but yeah, I wanted to walk Becca home. She went off to say goodbye to Judy and somebody and I looked around for Pat and Ron. I waved at Ron from across the room, giving him my best leer as Becca came back. She waved at Ron too. We collected our jackets and left just as Peter, Paul and Mary arrived, on the turntable of course.

The cold night air hit us both a semi-sobering lick when we reached the sidewalk on Marlborough street. Clumps of freshly plowed snow lined the streets and patches of silvery snow clung to the lawns and hedges along the way. The street lamps glowed golden and the walkways were clear. I put my arm around Becca. Becca put her arm around me. Life was good.

"Which way is home?" I asked, hoping she wouldn't say Connecticut.

"Just over on Newbury, up by the BPL," Becca answered. She and I were arm in arm, keeping warm, keeping close. "BPL" was cool Boston talk for the Boston Public Library. The streets around this landmark were lined with apartments, filled with thousands of college students, like us. We packed the restaurants, coffee shops, bars and lounges. There are sixteen major colleges and technical schools in the greater Boston area, upwards of twenty-five thousand students. We ruled the city.

"Are you living in town?" Becca asked.

"Lowell," I answered, "With my parents. I'm staying with friends for the weekend." This never sounded so uncool before.

"Well, you're staying with this friend, for this weekend," She replied with a very sexy twinkle in her eye. A gong rang inside me. I was at a loss for a snappy answer. Any answer. I hadn't exactly done what I think we were about to do before but as we walked along I figured there is a first time for everything. We walked a little faster.

Becca's apartment was in the obligatory three story walk up mid-way on Newbury Street. She was on the top floor, end of the hall. She used her key and let us in. The apartment was dark. She lit candles. There were posters on the walls, colorful rugs on the floors, big, feather-looking things in vases, and a sofa with an Afghan thrown over it in the living room. It smelled of patchouli.

"Take off your coat. Stay a while," She said as she busied herself around the room.  She had taken off her jacket, her scarf, her shoes.

"Want some wine?" She pulled a bottle of Mateus Rose out of the refrigerator. Unopened. There were corks and glasses to be dealt with. We settled onto the sofa. My heart was pounding like a hammer. I hoped it didn't show.

"Do you have roommates?' I asked, subtly gulping as much Mateus Rose as I could swallow.

"Judy will stay at her boyfriend's tonight. Anna may be home later. She won't bother us." Becca moved closer on the sofa. Kissing started. Lots of squirming. Little noises. Then Becca jumped up. She tugged me to my feet.

"C'mon." And started down the hall to her bedroom. I followed. I brought the wine.

The bedroom had a mattress on the floor. No box spring. Lots of blankets. Quilts. More candles. The poster above the bed was Theda Bara in her famous silver and black costume as Cleopatra. Becca slipped into her bathroom. I refilled my glass with the last of the Mateus. Gulped it down. Looked around the bedroom, collapsed onto the edge of the mattress and kicked off my shoes.

Becca came out of the bathroom. She was wearing this robe thing, very short, very shear, very unbuttoned. And nothing else. She walked over to the bed, smiled that very sexy smile I told you about before and pushed me onto my back. She went to work on my belt buckle like she had some previous experience with that procedure. My clothes came off, her robe disappeared and in a very short time I was panting for air on the bed. Becca lay next to me.

"Was that your first time?" She asked quietly.

"Yes," I half whispered, half embarrassed, half grateful, very grateful.

"Not bad," she grinned as she threw her leg over me. "But I guarantee you are going to like your second time even better."

And I did. Number three was pretty spectacular as well. Any more details would be bragging. The next morning Becca and I shared a granola like breakfast, grinning at each other across the kitchen table. Judy came home and Anna woke up. Neither seemed surprised to find me there.

I asked Becca what her plans were for the day, looking longingly down the hall toward her bedroom. She told me she was meeting her study group at the BPL at 11 and they would probably study until about three or four. Then she told me she had plans for Saturday night, some play she was going to with a friend. Gary. I got the drift. When she walked me to the door she gave me her phone number and asked me to call next week if I wanted to. I told her I did, and I would.

So there, at last, it was. I had passed the Donna Delancey "pretend sex" threshold, gone beyond the respectful, long distance, fading celibacy of my relationship with Margaret Mary and had my first full-on sexual encounter.

Life was good. I had learned a couple of important lessons. First, Go To Parties! You never know. I also learned, biologically, where all the moving parts went, and what to do when you get them all together. But last, and certainly not least, I learned I liked this intercourse business, a lot. And forty years of bad road, unseen by me as yet, rolled out ahead of me. Incidentally, Becca did mention that she used protection. The pill. She told me this over the granola. I wish I had been smart enough to wonder about this earlier and made a note to do so in the future. Mine, hers and whoever else that may involve.

I stepped out into the bright, sun-shiney Boston streets feeling perhaps a little more grown up and a lot farther away from a childhood rapidly receding into my past.

And then the radio in my head clicked on…

*Tonight you're mine, completely,*
*You give your love so sweetly,*
*Tonight the light of love is in your eyes,*
*But will you love me tomorrow?*

*Is this a lasting treasure?*
*Or just a moment's pleasure?*
*Can I believe the magic in your sighs?*
*Will you still love me tomorrow?*

*Tonight with words unspoken,*
*You say that I'm the only one.*
*But will my heart be broken,*
*When the night meets the morning sun?*

*I'd like to know that your love,*
*Is love I can be sure of,*
*So tell me now and I won't ask again,*
*Will you still love me tomorrow?*

But I could think about that later.

"Will You Love Me Tomorrow?", Written by Carole King and Gerry Goffin. Recorded by The Shirelles. It reached #1 on the Billboard charts in 1960, the first #1 hit by a black female singing group.

HON
EST
AS
ET
DILI
GEN
TIA
1906
SUFFOLK
UNIVERSITY
BOSTON
COLLEGE OF
ARTS & SCIENCES

# Chapter Fifteen

## *School Is Out (Boola Boola)*

My second semester at Suffolk University wasn't ending well. I had, for the most part, neglected my studies. I did enough to keep my head above water, study, memorize, repeat, but little else. I spent most of my time hanging around the student union, playing low stakes poker between, and sometimes during classes, shooting a little pool at the student union and living at Jimmy's on weekends. I wasn't drifting anymore, I was standing still, getting stagnant.

Earlier this month Teddy asked me to meet him down at Lefty's. When I got there Teddy was at a table in the back and it looked like he had something to say.

"I'm doin' it," he announced as soon as I sat down.

"Doing what?" I answered. Teddy sounded a little nervous, his voice mixing bravado with uncertainty.

"I joined up, signed the papers today. I'm going in the Marine Corps."

I was surprised, not stunned but surprised. I knew Teddy was thinking about enlisting but I thought he and I would talk a little more about it before he made the decision.

"When?" Was all I could stammer.

"A week from today. Sergeant Woods fixed it all up for me."

"You tell your father yet? What did he say?"

"Haven't told him yet. Connie neither. Nobody knows except you."

"Geez, Ted, what made you decide to do this?"

"Chris is home, not here home, he's in San Diego. He got wounded. A telegram came to the house the day before yesterday. It said he was gonna' be alright but he'll be in the hospital for a while."

"Was he hurt bad? Did they say?"

"Only that he was in the hospital and would be in touch in a few days. Connie went nuts, started yellin' at my father, sayin' this was all his fault. My father stayed down at the garage last night, didn't even come home. When I saw him today he looked sadder than I ever saw him before, even after my Mother died."

"What do you think he's going to say when he finds out you enlisted?"

"I don't know, I ain't tellin' him. I'll tell Connie before I go and let her tell him."

I hated seeing Teddy this way. All the time he was talking he stared at the table top and barely looked me in the eye. Then he looked up and whispered, "I didn't know what to do so I joined up."

On the day he was to be inducted I took the day off from school and rode with Teddy into Boston where he would be sent off to Parris Island. We were quiet most of the train ride in. Teddy seemed apprehensive, more than a little scared, but determined to see his decision through. I was worried, worried about losing my best friend, worried that he could be hurt or killed, worried that he was making a decision I should have made with him. He was going. I was staying. I wondered which of us had made the right decision.

When we shook hands to say goodbye I gave Teddy a package which had eight envelopes in it. They all had stamps and were made out to my address and his father's. This was my mother's idea and I thought it was a good one.

"Write to me and let me know how you're doing okay?" I said with a lump in my throat.

"Yeah," Teddy answered. His throat might have been lumpy too.

Teddy had been gone about a month when Margaret Mary called me on a Sunday night to say she was not coming home for the summer. She was going to intern at a food bank and community center in Cicero and take two summer semester courses. She sounded very excited, very involved. I told her that sounded great.  It wasn't.

Lately my communication with Margaret Mary had involved a lot of talk about some guy named Kendall. Kendall was taking her to a lecture, Kendall had tickets to a concert, she was going with him. Kendall wrote poetry. Kendall played guitar. Kendall sounded like an asshole.

Of course I had the whole Becca situation to not discuss with Margaret Mary. I had seen her two more times since that first night. We hadn't slept together on either occasion. Turned out she has a Kendall too, only his name is Brent. Becca was polite about it and all but it was plain Brent was going to be filling the role I wished I was filling. It's not like I had great feelings for Becca other than lust, but lust being what it is I wasn't happy about this turn of events either.

That's what my life was like when I met Jimmy in the cafeteria after our final final exam. I had just lied my way through an appreciation of literature course and Jimmy was wrapping up year one of law school. Neither of us appeared very triumphant at our accomplishment.

"I hate this place! I'm quitting!" Jimmy slammed his text books down on the cafeteria table. His face was red, his voice strained, his hands were shaking.

"Jimmy, what the hell happened?" The guy looked like he was going to have a heart attack. I was trying to calm him down.

"You know what? Shakespeare was right! Shakespeare was a genius! He had the only good idea I've heard at this place since I got here." Jimmy was steaming and I knew exactly what he was talking about.

*"The first thing we do, let's kill all the lawyers!"* Jimmy quoted emphatically.

It's a line from Henry VI, Part 2, Act IV, Scene 2. I might not have learned much here this year, but I did learn Shakespeare. Nothing about my first year of college surprised me more or brought me more happiness than getting to know and understand Shakespeare. I must tell you about how this happened.

"Shakespeare 101, Introduction to the Plays" was a required course for Journalism majors. What little I had learned about this guy from high school had to do with some mostly unintelligible gibberish like, "To be or not to be, that is the question." I never found out the answer.

Then there was, "Romeo, Romeo, Wherefore art thou Romeo? Wherefore art thou?" Really?

I also could mostly recall, "Beware the Ides of March" but had no idea when the Ides of March were or who should beware of them.

That was about it for Lowell High School Shakespeare. Outside class I preferred Mark Twain and Mickey Spillane. Then, here at Suffolk I took the mandatory class taught by Mrs. Herman, Gloria Herman to her students. Her passion for Shakespeare was sincere, her knowledge of his works all-encompassing, her class was enchanting. As I struggled with the "wouldeth's" and "Hath's", the "maketh's" and "doth's" that seemed to ramble on forever I confessed to Gloria I could not find the magic in Shakespeare's words. And she suggested a magical thing.

"Go to the library," she said, "Check out the recorded plays of Shakespeare from the London Theatre group. Let Lawrence Olivier speak to you as Hamlet, John Gielgud as King Lear, both were knighted for their efforts you know, hear Dame Judith Anderson's interpretation of Lady Macbeth and you must know Paul Robeson's marvelous Othello."

This amazing lady literally squirmed with delight as she rattled of these names and plays. I barely knew any of these guys or dames, but nodded my head wisely as if I did.

Then I did something right. I went to the library, found the Long Playing records of these plays and listened, with headphones, as I read. It was as if the words went from black and white to full, glorious color. The diction, the inflection, the pace, the tone cleared away the fog in my head and I heard, and understood and appreciated the wonderment I was hearing. If I got nothing else out of my first stab at college (and I didn't) I got this. So that's how I knew about killing all the lawyers.

"You know what Professor Beche told my "Introduction to Criminal Defense" class are the two most important legal terms we would learn this semester?"

Jimmy was still huffing and puffing, though he had managed to plop himself into a chair.

I, of course, had no idea what he was talking about.

Jimmy continued, "He said they were "Retainer" and "Continuance"! He was laughing when he said it. You know what the seniors call Beche's class? "Bleed 'em and plead 'em.!"

"Beche says in the majority of criminal defense cases an attorney, at best, functions as part of the financially punitive process."

"I have no idea what that means," I said as Jimmy magically produced a package of Hostess Sno-Ball cupcakes from his briefcase.

"Statistically as many as seventy-five percent of a criminal defense lawyers clients are guilty of whatever they have been charged with, or something close. That is why they need a criminal defense lawyer in the first place. You ever had a criminal defense lawyer?" Jimmy asked, popping the pink Sno-Ball into his mouth.

I told him I hadn't.

"That's because you're not a criminal!" Jimmy shouted as heads in the cafeteria turned. He lowered his voice. "I don't want to spend my life around people who are seventy-five percent guilty of something!"

"Sounds like criminal law isn't for you Jimmy." I was trying to be the voice of reason.

"I just took an exam where I wrote a contract nobody on earth could possibly understand and I know I gave the absolutely correct answer."

Jimmy stared at the white cupcake and said, sadly, "You know what I learned most about becoming a lawyer this year? I learned how much I didn't want to be a lawyer."

"So what are you going to do, Jimmy? This isn't going to play well with your parents."

I had met Jimmy's parents at the beginning of the year when they came up to Boston to check on Jimmy's progress. They weren't checking on Jimmy, just his progress.

"I've been talking to my brother. He says I can come live with him in New York City if I want to." Jimmy made his answer sound like a question.

Jimmy, it turned out has an older brother, Wayne. Wayne had attended two years at Suffolk, then quit and moved to New York. Dad and Mom disowned him. Seems he wanted to study art, sculpture to be exact. A "pansy artist" according to Jimmy's father.

"What would you do in New York?" I asked, besides make your father the angriest human being on the planet, I didn't add.

"Wayne has his own studio now. Last month he sold a sculpture for three thousand dollars. He said if I decide to come, I shouldn't worry about the money."

"Wow, that's some brother."

"Kind of balances out my father," Jimmy replied, unhappily.

"What you should maybe do," I offered, "is think about it for a while. Don't do anything quick you might regret later."

"You mean like going to law school?" Jimmy managed a laugh.

"Jim, I'm kind of in the same boat, only without the older brother. I don't know whether I'm going to stay here or not either. But I'm going to give it a lot of thought over the summer. How about you do the same thing and we get together in a few weeks and talk about it?"

I was very good at procrastination.

"Okay," Jimmy replied, "How about I come up here for that Fourth of July concert down on the Charles and we talk about it then?"

"Fourth of July it is, Jimmy. Count on it."

So Jimmy gobbled the white Sno-Ball, I finished my coffee and our first semester at Suffolk came to an end.

Before we packed up and left school that day I offered Jimmy one more line from Shakespeare, one I was going to have to give a lot of thought to in the next few weeks. The line is from a guy named Polonius, in Hamlet, Act 1, Scene III,

*"This is above all,*
*to your own self be true,*
*And it must follow,*
*as the night the day,*
*Thou cans't not then be false*
*to any man."*

Even myself.

Perhaps.

# Chapter Sixteen

## *Hot August Fight*

"Ball three!" The umpire shouted.

Low and outside, a must take pitch that made the count 3-1.

Now I had to get a strike, a hitter's pitch, or else the pitcher was going to walk me, which, if he did, I would steal second on his first move to the plate and be in scoring position for Steve Welch, the hottest hitter on our team.

We were down one run and this was our last at bat. There were two outs. This was playoff baseball, first round of the Middlesex Valley regional championship, a big deal. The Lowell Phillies, that was my team, against the Lawrence Pirates. The game was being played under the lights at Grissom Park and a large crowd was in attendance. My Mom and Dad were there, of course, as were, my two younger brothers, Bob and John, along with a crowd of aunts and uncles, cousins and neighbors.

I stepped out of the batter's box and rubbed some dirt on my hands. I didn't need the dirt, I was just letting the pitcher sweat a little. Nervous time, for him and me. More for him, I hoped.

I stepped back into the batter's box and the pitcher, Mike Adams, went into his windup. High and outside. I dropped my bat and headed for first base.

"Strike Two!" The umpire shouted. I stopped, looked at the ump who had a "don't you dare say anything" look on his face. I turned around, picked up my bat and got back in the box. That pitch was ball four, the ump must be blind. I heard a scattered boo or two from the crowd, and then locked in on the pitcher. Three and two, the big one due, went the baseball rhyme. I waited for the next pitch.

"Nice goin' Ferrier! You lost the game for us!" Fat Jerry Kovac was in my face once again. This time we were teammates, supposedly, on the Connie Mack League Phillies, who had just been eliminated from the playoffs. My strikeout was the final out. Mike Adams had thrown me a killer curveball. I eyed it up and got ready to hammer it when it broke like it fell off a tabletop. I missed it by a mile. Good pitch, great pitch. I tipped my hat as the ump hollered, "Strike Three!" That to me was what baseball was all about. You played hard, played to win, but when the other team makes a great play you tip your hat. Sportsmanship was the proverb, here. But not for Jerry Kovac.

"Way to make us lose!" Jerry continued, stomping along beside me as I walked to the bat rack. Jerry was our back up catcher, a lump and a loudmouth. I could never figure how he made the team in the first place. He didn't play much and not very well when he did. I tried to ignore him as I put down my bat but he shoved me from behind and I stumbled into the bat rack and onto the ground. Jerry stood over me laughing.

Our coach, Billy Devine, was across the field talking to the other coach and didn't see what happened. What he did see was me jump up and slam Jerry in the stomach, a good right hand with lots of shoulder behind it. Jerry folded in half, staggered backward, wooshing for breath and trying to keep his balance. And that is where this whole thing should have ended. But it didn't.

I put a lot of anger into that punch, only some of it had anything to do with Jerry Kovac. My best friend had disappeared into the Marine Corps five months ago and I hadn't heard from him since. Margaret Mary was spending the summer in Chicago and there was the whole Kendall thing. Only last week Jimmy Barone moved to New York City to live with his brother. He would not be coming back to Suffolk in the fall. He told me he was going to enroll in a culinary arts school. He wanted to be a chef. The guy loved to be around food.

I was living at home, trying to stay out of everybody's way, brooding a lot, my new favorite hobby, and generally making myself miserable. I was working a few shifts at Lefty's but the magic of filling coke cups and making frappes and milkshakes had faded.

Earlier that summer the President had announced we were stepping up our bombing of Hanoi and Haiphong in North Vietnam. US Troop strength in South Vietnam continued to increase. Casualty lists grew longer. In Chicago, where Margaret Mary was, a monster by the name of Richard Speck murdered eight student nurses in their dormitory one bloody summer night. Then in Texas, only a few days later, a madman named Charles Whitman murdered his wife and mother, drove to the University of Texas at Austin and climbed into a bell tower where he killed thirteen people and wounded thirty one more with a sniper rifle before blowing his own brains out.

Around the country the police and National Guard were turning fire hoses on anti-war protestors. The House Un-American Activities Committee announced it would begin investigations into protestors who were giving aid to the Viet Cong.

I looked hard for sanity anywhere I could find it. Old pleasures were fading, familiar faces were disappearing, hard times weren't coming, they seemed to be everywhere. I walked the mile long stretch of Long Sands Beach in York, Maine over and over and for the first time in my life I felt lonely there.

So as not to miss a single rung on my personal downward ladder of self-pity and despair I started reading Poe. Yes, Edgar Allen Poe, American madman, inebriate and genius. I reveled not only in the Pits and the Pendulums, the Masques of Red Death and Murderers of the Rue Morgue but in his often addled thoughts which I adopted for my own.

*"And being so young
and dipped in folly,
I fell in love with melancholy."*

Even better,

*"I felt that I had breathed an
atmosphere of sorrow."*

And not even finally,

*"And all I loved, I loved alone."*

This guy was becoming my new imaginary best friend. With apologies to Mr. Twain.

Then a bolt of even less sunshine oozed from the AM radio. A song, a dirge perfect for me in my present state. It goes like this,

*A winter's day, In a deep and dark December,*
*I am alone,*
*Gazing from my window to the streets below*
*On a freshly fallen silent shroud of snow,*
*I am a Rock, I am an Island.*

*I've built walls, a fortress deep and mighty,*
*That no one can penetrate,*
*I have no need of friendship*
*Friendship causes pain.*
*It's laughter and it's loving I disdain.*
*I am a Rock, I am an Island.*

> Don't talk of love, I've heard the word before,
> It's sleeping in my memory,
> I can't disturb the slumber of
> feelings that have died,
> If I never loved, I never would have cried,
> I am a Rock, I am an Island.
>
> I have my books, and my poetry to protect me,
> I am shielded in my armor,
> Hiding in my room, safe within my womb,
> I touch no one and no one touches me,
> I am a Rock, I am an Island.
>
> And a Rock feels no pain,
> And an Island never cries.

Move on over Edgar Allen Poe. Hello Paul Simon.

I was a basket case.

Now I couldn't even enjoy baseball anymore. I loved baseball. I had played every summer since Little League. I learned how to play properly and become a good teammate. I could bat, catch and throw with the best of them. It was fun, win or lose, and I enjoyed every inning. Until this summer and the Connie Mack League.

Connie Mack League followed Babe Ruth League. Ages were 17 through 19. There were fewer teams in the league, so fewer players. Better players, better competition. And that is where things started to go wrong for me.

When I made the Phillies I was proud. The guys I was playing with were the best in town. So were the guys I was playing against. Winning was important but playing well was what it was all about for me. One team is always going to lose. If you did your best and the other team was better, so be it. If your team got a bad break, it would probably get a lucky bounce or a good break later on. Winning wasn't the point. Playing my best game was. This isn't what I came up against that summer. I was used to having coaches advise me, coach me, teach me. Billy Devine was a screamer, a yeller. Guys are going to boot ground balls, not catch up to fly balls, strike out, that's part of the game. But when something like that happened Billy Devine would blow his stack, yell and scream, suck all the fun out of the game.

"Winning isn't everything," he'd say, "BUT NOT LOSING IS!" He would roar at team meetings.

He'd clap and be happy on the good plays, congratulate us when we did something right, but hell and damnation followed any miscue, most strikeouts, all losses. We were 12-2 that summer, but all we heard about were the two losses. Close games, well played. Unacceptable to Coach Devine. And Jerry Kovac.

All season long Jerry had been a pain in the ass. Everything I did he complained he could do better. But couldn't. When he did get in a game he was tub of lard slow on the basepaths, a pop-up hitter who occasionally, but not very occasionally, got hold of a long ball, a late innings catcher when the game wasn't close. All that with a big mouth and a bad attitude.

But Coach Devine seemed to like him. That made one of us.

I was sick of this crap by mid-season and wanted to quit. The games were not fun anymore. We won a lot more than we lost but even winning wasn't fun. There was more gloating than respecting, more disrespect than sportmanship.

I talked to my about all this with my Dad and he told me I should finish the season. "Winners never quit," he said. He told me I was a winner.

From across the field a victory chant went up and a few of the Pirate's players were laughing and flipping us off. Insults were tossed as both coaches tried to settle down the shoddy winners.

And just about then Jerry straightened up, still gasping for air. He was trying to mutter a string of obscenities but couldn't catch his breath. He took a stumbling step toward me and I should have walked away. But I didn't.

Jerry took another step toward me, cursing as he came, and before I could think it through I stepped into Jerry and hit him square on the jaw with a cross-over right hand that completely put his lights out. I felt the crunch when I slammed Jerry's face. It turned out I broke his jaw in two places. He was flat on the ground when Steve Welch pulled me away and coach Devine came running across the field.

"What the hell is going on here?" He bellowed as he knelt beside Jerry.

"He started it," was all I could manage to say as a crowd formed around us and Doc Ryan, a league official who came to all our games, examined Jerry.

"This boy is seriously injured," he pronounced while scowling at me. "He's going to need to be taken to the hospital."

And that, along with the aftermath, ended my baseball career. Jerry's jaw needed to be wired shut. It would heal over time, my reputation wouldn't.

I got kicked of the team, of course. I deserved it. I apologized to Jerry and to my now ex-teammates. Jerry's parents were furious and wanted to have me arrested. Jerry's well known reputation as a bully and a loudmouth bailed me out. Others had seen him push me over the bat rack. The league insurance picked up the medical bills and the incident, if not the circumstances, were forgotten, though not forgiven.

I recall driving with my Dad to the league office two days later to turn in my uniform. There was a heavy, gloomy silence in the car until he asked, "What happened, son. That was not like you."

I wasn't so sure. In fact I wasn't so sure exactly what I was like these days. Most of the time I was unhappy, the rest of the time I was miserable. I couldn't seem to shake the black cloud that hung over me, and recently I had stopped trying very hard to do so.

This was not the way I wanted to end my baseball playing days. But it was. The "not quite a fight" I had with Jerry was the last time I would ever get to wear a baseball uniform, or play in an organized league or tip my hat to a better player. I went out wrong after years and years of playing the game right. I let Jerry Kovac take that away from me and I had a whole new paragraph of things I didn't like about myself.

As for what I told my father that day in the car all I could say is that I was sorry and I truly was. Further reflection would reveal that losing baseball was not the only thing I was sorry about. I was sorry I was allowing others, even my Mom and Dad to decide what was the right thing for me to be doing. I had more than enough of classrooms, teachers, tests and term papers. I wanted to do something else, even if it was the wrong thing, it would at last be something I had chosen myself. But so far I didn't have the courage to come right out and say this. It was easier to go along.

Until Jerry Kovac.

"Dad, I don't want to go back to school in the fall."

I finally worked up the courage to say it as we drove home from the league office. My Dad looked over at me and just for a moment I saw that expression on his face I dreaded most in the world, disappointment. I probably could have picked a better time for this conversation but the words burst out before I could stop them. I felt relieved, and then I felt miserable.

My Dad didn't answer at first. What he did do was pull into the parking lot of Paradise Donuts. We went inside and got a table, two coffees and two donuts. Most days this would have been terrific. Not so much today.

"What is the problem with school, son?" My Dad asked.

"I don't feel like I'm learning anything Dad. I'm memorizing a lot of stuff, repeating it back, doing what they tell me I'm supposed to do and not doing anything I think I'm supposed to do."

My Dad was a good listener. He didn't interrupt, he didn't comment or judge. He waited for me to finish.

"And what is it you feel you should be doing that you're not?"

Now we were into the hard stuff. I chewed my donut a little longer than necessary while trying to formulate a decent answer. Finally I swallowed and said, "I'm not sure, Dad, but I know it's not sitting in a classroom all day. I just don't see the purpose."

"Sometime," he answered, "we do things that don't seem to have much purpose at the time but they pay off later. I spent six years in night school to get my degree and then I got a good job down at Haartz Auto because I had that degree."

When I was little I recall my father coming home from work at suppertime, eating with us and then going back out again after dark to ride a bus cross-town to night school at Lowell Technological Institute. I had no idea what he was studying there, only that he did not return home again until long after our bed time and that he left again for work early in the morning while we were still having breakfast. I vaguely recall him studying at the kitchen table on weekends and being told to stay out of there so he could concentrate. So naturally my brothers and I hung around the kitchen doorway until he finally put down his books and invited us in to bounce on his knee.

"Didn't you ever get tired of it, Dad?' I wondered.

"Of course I did, but I wanted a better life for all of us and I knew that would come with a better job that I could have with a better education. There's lots of jobs where you'll make a living, college can give you a job where you have a future."

"What kind of future, Dad? I got the draft breathing down my neck, Teddy's already gone, lots of my other friends are already in the service or are getting ready to go in, and I'm hiding in school while they go off to war."

"You feel like you should be going off to war?" My Dad didn't sound like he disapproved, he sounded like he understood.

"You did," I responded.

All my life I had secretly thrilled at poring through the old footlocker in the cellar which held my Dad's WWII memorabilia. There were sepia brown photographs of him in gunnery school training down in Texas, his leather flight helmet with communication wires still attached, fur lined leather gloves, notebooks, maps and his framed Honorable Discharge.

Whenever he became aware that my brothers and I had been rummaging through his mementos he'd gently ask us to close up the box and not play with them. They seemed to make him sad somehow. They made me proud.

"That war was about stopping Hitler, about avenging Pearl Harbor, I'm not sure what the hell this damn war is all about son."

This was a big deal. My father NEVER swore. It was like Rhett Butler at the end of Gone With The Wind. The whole world was shocked when Rhett said he didn't give a damn. I was shocked now. My father had said "Hell" and "Damn" in the same sentence! A first.

My father, you see, was a patriot. Like Sergeant Woods he believed with his whole heart in Duty, Honor, Country. So did I through war movie after war movie, weekly television shows like Combat!, 12 O'Clock High, The Gallant Men and The Rat Patrol, even farces like Hogan's Heroes and McHales Navy, we were the good guys, we did the right thing. And now my father wasn't so sure about "this damn war."

Such was the notion sweeping across the country, dividing us in two. Spearheaded on the college campuses but spreading into the suburbs as the military graveyards filled up.

"I want you to do me a favor son. For me and for your mother."

There was no way I was going to say no to this, no matter what it was.

"Give Suffolk another try. Fall semester. Then we will talk more about this. I want you to do what you think is right, I just don't want you to do something in a hurry you may regret later. Deal?"

Of course it was a deal. We clinked donuts on it. I actually felt better than I had in quite some time. I'd give it the old college try, for them, and for me.

And in a few short weeks I'd be back at school, repeating things I didn't need to know, doing things I didn't need to do, but thinking about it a lot.

*He runs the bases like a choo-choo train,*
*Swings 'round second like an aeroplane,*
*His cap flies off when he passes third,*
*And heads for home like an eagle bird.*
*Say hey, say who?*
*Say Willie.*
*That Giant's kid is great.*

And that's the way it is supposed to be.

# Chapter Seventeen

## School Days

## (Education At Last)

"Wanna shoot some 9 ball?"

I looked up from the red felt pool table in the Suffolk University Student Union and first laid my eyes upon a guy who would soon become my new best buddy, mentor, guide and downfall.

"My name's Eddie, Eddie Legrand," the stranger offered me his hand.

Grinning at me with a cheerful, friendly smile was a guy about my age, blond haired, crew cut, dressed in a very preppy blue and white seersucker shirt, white chinos, saddle shoes and holding a two piece, custom made pool cue.

Now Lowell may not have prepared me much for big city ways, but I had learned never to play pool with strangers carrying a custom pool cue no matter how friendly, or preppy they appeared.

"Eddie" looked to me like Joe College himself, or a guy selling very expensive golf clubs at the country club. Very congenial, very low key, but there was that custom pool cue.

"You shoot a good stick. How 'bout a buck on the five, deuce on the nine?"

Fast. Fast Eddie. I had heard that name somewhere before.

"No thanks. I've got a class in ten minutes. Just going to finish this rack, then you can have the table."

"Class huh? Watcha' got?" "Eddie" wasn't giving up.

"Rhetoric, Professor Quincy's class," I answered as the last ball of my rack rolled in.

"Yeah, Quincy, crazy old bastard. I took that class last year. Buncha' bullshit. Got an "A" though."

"You're a student here?" You meet all kinds.

"Junior, sort of. I'm on like a sabbatical, auditin' a couple of classes for now."

"Good for you, I have to go. Enjoy your game." I racked my cue, grabbed my books and headed for the door.

"Yeah sure, I'm just here practicin' you know? See you around some time."

Eddie grabbed the nine ball rack and began expertly stacking the balls, checking out the room for another player. I had seen this guy around the game room before. Usually he was hustling some victim out of his milk money, playing just well enough to win and occasionally dropping a shot that didn't look like amazing luck.

I stayed around long enough to watch Eddie crack the break on the nine ball rack and pocket three balls on bank shots that took a lot of practice. Eddie could shoot at a level nobody else in the room was even close to. If he was practicing anything it was not to give away how good he was. I left the game room to practice staying awake in Professor Quincy's rhetoric class, then took my usual 4:10 train from North Station to Lowell.

The Winchester, Wedgemere, Wilmington, and North Billerica train stations clicked by while I read the sports pages of the Record American and watched the sun go down outside the coach window. My daily commute to and from Boston had become somewhat of a dreary routine. The novelty of the ride into North Station, the short walk through the Boston streets to Suffolk University and the rhythm of college classes was wearing thin.

The fall sophomore semester at Suffolk was marginally more interesting than my freshman year. I took another Shakespeare course with the glorious Gloria Herman. I had previously encountered the histories, the dramas, parts of the sonnets and was now experiencing "A Midsummer's Night Dream," "As You Like it," "Twelvth Night" and "The Taming of the Shrew." Good stuff, worth the price of admission.

A good deal of my deep summer gloom had lifted. I met a girl named Susan, who was much like Becca, only without the boyfriend. She lived at home with her parents as I did, which led to some lively frolicking at Jimmy's old apartment when Ron and Ted were out on the town and we weren't. The rent was still a case of beer, well within my budget.

So far college was high school with a longer reading list and sex. By second semester I was going through the motions, getting by, getting bored and doing nothing about it.

"Hiya, didn't catch your name last time." Two days later I was back at the student union game room, Eddie was there as well, sipping a coke, pool cue in hand. I was running a couple of racks between classes.

"Dave," I replied, lining up a shot. The four ball dropped cleanly into the side pocket leaving me position on the seven.

"Nice," Eddie nodded. "Wanna' shoot some?"

I straightened up and looked across the table at Eddie. He was chalking his cue.

"Eddie, just so we're clear. I don't play for money and I've watched you around here. You make shots I don't even see and I see a lot of shots."

Up in Lowell I was a pretty good pool player. The Sears & Roebuck pool table in our basement at Glenmere Street had given me many enjoyable hours of practice. My Uncle Artie was a flat out pool shark who taught me and my brothers how to hold the cue, make a bridge, draw the cue ball, play position and see the table. I was good. Eddie was better, quite a bit better.

"You're holdin' your back elbow too high. Punchin' down on the ball a little. Throws you off on your follow through," Eddie commented.

I took a moment to consider. Maybe there was something I could learn from this guy.

"You play eight ball?" I asked.

"Does the pope shit where the bears eat breakfast?" Eddie answered moving quickly to the table and re-racking the scattered balls.

"No dough, Eddie, I am, as they say, without funds."

"Don't sweat it. We'll just practice, you know, for fun."

Eddie then proceeded to beat me four straight games. And I knew he wasn't showing me his best game.

"Ya gotta keep that elbow down, and hit 'em like they was eggs," Eddie offered after my latest defeat. "Not bad though, that was a nice combo on the eleven."

"Sometimes I get lucky."

"Nah, it ain't luck. Practice. Practice and concentration. Ya' gotta' want to win, or need to win." Eddie was teaching. It was about time I started learning something in college.

About that time two Kappa Sig frat guys walked in. They were the hale and hearty college types, ten dollar haircuts, tan chinos and navy blue windbreakers with gold Greek letters on the front pocket. They were looking for a pool table. Eddie offered them ours. Sort of.

"Hey, you guys wanna' play?" He offered cheerfully. "Little eight ball, we can play partners."

The frat boys looked at each other and nodded. They were Todd and Mike. They selected cues from the rack. Eddie shot me a wolf grin and let them break. We then proceeded to lose the first two games. Eddie dumped shots I knew he could have made in his sleep. He acted very disappointed in himself. Todd and Mike were on a roll.

"Geez, I can't believe how bad I'm playin'," Eddie moaned. "Any of you guys want a Coke?"

Eddie came back to the table carrying four cokes. We chatted for a while. Todd and Mike were pre-law. Corporate and contracts, bonds and securities. Eddie left out the "sabbatical" part of his status, saying he was a first semester junior, undeclared as yet. Todd and Mike were very condescending of my freshman journalism status.

"It's not too late to change," Mike offered, "Journalism is a good way to end up driving used cars for the rest of your life." That got a good laugh from Todd. Eddie laughed too, then he said,

"Hey, you want to play buck a man? Make it interesting?"

Forty-five minutes later Eddie and I were up five bucks each. Todd and Mike were starting to get uneasy.

"Hey, I gotta' split," Eddie announced. "Got a class. You got one too, don't ya' Dave?"

I nodded. We shook hands with Todd and Mike. Money was exchanged. Eddie and I left the student union.

As we walked away I said, "Eddie, don't put me in those situations, OK? I may not have the money to handle my end."

"No sweat," he replied, "I'll cover ya' if that ever happens, only that ain't ever gonna' happen."

"You sure of that?"

"Candy from babies," he laughed, "Look, five bucks is pennies to these guys. Trust fund babies living on an allowance my old man never saw in his twenty years in the shipyards. You wanna' grab a cup of coffee?"

Next thing I knew I was at the Travis Coffee shop in Copley Square. Very "in" college type hangout, downstairs, off the street. Exclusive.

Eddie greeted the counterman, "Joe," who shot him a grin and handed him a brown envelope. Eddie worked the room saying "hi" to several tables-full of people as he grabbed us a corner slot.

"So where you from?" Eddie asked as a waitress delivered two unordered cups of coffee and two bagels, cream cheese and chopped onion. I considered the chow as Eddie scooped up a bagel and started slathering cheese and onion.

"Lowell," I answered and gave him the five minute history.

"How you liking Suffolk?" He asked, chewing bagel.

One thing I noticed over the ensuing conversation is that Eddie's eyes never stopped moving over the room. He watched close and he listened close as I told him I was just kind of drifting along at school not sure if I wanted to be there.

"Yeah, lotsa' guys say that, don't worry about it. It'll either kick in or it won't. College ain't for everybody."

I was seriously starting to think I was one of those everybody's.

I tried the bagel. No onion. Tasty and toasty.

"Do you mind if I ask you something?" I said between bagel crunches. Eddie bobbed his head, chewing. Looked like a "go ahead."

"Why did you pick me out for the hustle the other day? Do I look like a victim to you?"

Eddie put down his bagel and considered me carefully. "Two reasons," he began, "First, you shoot a pretty good stick. I figured you'd give me a little competition."

"A little?" I laughed.

"Some, like I said, good stick. Second, I watched you play for a while. You were enjoyin' yourself. Relaxin'. Most guys are just banging balls around, showin' off, foolin' around. It's an insult to the game."

"And that offends you?" I asked, half serious, half joking.

"Look, I don't shoot pool to play around, I shoot to make money. That's what I do, I make money." Eddie sat back in his chair, stared at me.

"Is that why you called me in against Todd and Mike?"

"Sure, takes two to take two. Besides, I figured you could use the dough."

This time I sat back, deciding whether to be offended or amused. Having other people decide whether or not I could use money was not to my liking.

Eddie continued, "Another thing, you were straight up with me about playing for money. Didn't try to bullshit me, just said you didn't gamble for money and," Eddie grinned, "you spotted my hustle right off."

"But next thing I knew you had me gambling for money." I laughed, not that I fought the proposition too hard.

"Shooting pool with me is not gambling," Eddie replied, "shooting pool against me is gambling." He laughed back and picked up his bagel. This could be the start of a beautiful friendship.

Eddie went on to explain that he was not a junior at Suffolk, he was not a student at Suffolk. Or at any other college. He hung out there though, as well as at nearby Emerson College and across town at Boston University and occasionally across the Charles River at Harvard.

Eddie admitted he was a full time gambler, campus variety. "Lotta' money in those book bags," Eddie chuckled.

Pool was not his only game. He also hawked weekly sports betting cards on all four campuses, scalped tickets to the Celtics, Bruins and Red Sox to the local gentry and played poker, whist and cribbage with the willing and over educated. He never won too much, had lots of friends, customers and victims on each campus, and even occasionally lost a little money to them to balance the scales of his credibility.

"There's a guy over at Harvard beggin' me to play him for five hundred bucks," Eddie claimed, "Can't do it though, I'd beat him like a gong, but that would ruin me on "The Yahd". I take down more than that in smaller pieces every month over there. Never shear a sheep to the bone. Leave 'em a little dignity. People would rather believe they were unlucky than stupid."

Eddie was born and raised in Chelsea, across the Tobin Bridge and adjacent to the Boston Naval shipyards. The shipyards employed the bulk of the population living in the area, swallowed them up and never let go. His father, he explained, had been a welder there, twenty-three years. He died three years earlier from mesothelioma, too many hours of overtime and three packs of Camel cigarettes a day. What Eddie remembered most about his father were the burn scars.

"My old man," Eddie related, "the backs of his hands, his forearms, sides of his neck even, were covered with these burn marks, hundreds of them. Got them from the sparks from the welder's torch. He was proud of them, wore them like badges. So did all his friends. My old man was forty-two when he died. Ninety pounds he weighed at the end. I ain't gonna' end up like that."

His mother, "Ma" he called her, was still at the same apartment she shared with her husband and son for twenty-five years. She had never worked outside the home. She had never cashed her own paycheck, driven a car or been beyond the Boston city limits. That sort of thing just wasn't done. Not then, not in Chelsea. Eddie lived with her, there were no brothers or sisters, and he paid the bulk of the bills.

"My old man, he didn't leave much. He was a hard worker, for sure, but what he didn't owe, he spent at the bar with my Ma, Wiggins Tavern. When I was a little kid I thought it was like another room in our house. Weird, huh?"

I was fascinated. Sitting in a very fashionable college coffee shop, munching a bagel with a guy who looked like he just walked out of a pep rally and hearing about his father's burn scars and mother's lifelong seclusion was a window into a world I never knew existed. I was realizing there was much more to learn in Boston than Suffolk University was ever going to teach me.

"My Ma," Eddie continued, "doesn't want me to end up in the ship yard like my father."

"She didn't like that he worked there?" I asked.

"Nah, it isn't that. She just wants more for me, you know?"

I didn't know, but I was finding out. In Boston's inner city neighborhoods generations, great-grandfather deep lived and worked and married and died on the same street, often in the same tenement. Trades such as ship yard workers, railroad employees, postman, butchers, bakers and police were family affairs. Rigid and time honored pathways.

By the time he reached high school Eddie realized if he didn't think of a plan he was on a greased chute right into the Navy yard. High school was the end of the education line for almost all the kids from his neighborhood. Those who didn't enter the shipyard, entered the service. The Marine Corps was the service of choice. Tough kids, tough guys, tough Marines. Eddie wanted more. He had done well in school, made good grades, liked learning. History and math, he said, were his favorites. Nobody ever suggested college as an option for him though. Chelsea kids didn't much go to any of Boston's many colleges. "I told my teachers I wanted to take the College Boards," he recalled. "They said, 'What for?' I took 'em anyway. Got accepted at a coupla' places. Suffolk, BU, but I didn't have the money to go there. My Pop, he said he'd make it work somehow, you know? But it was like a couple of grand we weren't even close to havin'. I wasn't gonna put him into that kind of hole."

Eddie found work in the neighborhoods. He ran bets for the local bookies, barbers and bartenders, sold tout sheets at the racetracks, Suffolk Downs and Raynham Park, put a few of his own dollars on the street as loans to the local gambling degenerates and learned his way around pool and poker tables. Eddie was proud of the fact that he always played the game straight up, never cheated, only sheared the sheep with enough wool to take the shearing.

"People like to gamble, you know? The excitement, whatever. I like it too, but I like to win even more. Need to, you know? This is how I make my living."

The waitress refilled our coffee, twice, while students came by and dropped off betting cards and cash with Eddie. It was all very congenial. Eddie called them by name, even offered a tip or two when asked. He was street level business with a smile, entrepreneurship at its best.

"How long have you been doing this?" I asked, more than impressed with the whole operation.

"Coupla' years, built the business up slow, you know?"

"No college?"

"I audit classes sometime. Lecture halls mostly. Nobody keeps score of who's there. I sit in, take notes, even take the exams sometime. Nothing official though. Who needs it, I'm doin' okay?" Eddie answered offhandedly, but not entirely truthfully.

After that afternoon I became Eddie's pool shooting partner at Suffolk. We'd meet up at the student union on Tuesday and Thursday afternoon and I'd stick around until it was time for the late train to Lowell that evening. He played a lot of solo games but whenever a partners offer came up Eddie would stake us and off we'd go. My game was steady but not spectacular. His was lucky, very skillfully luck. Sometimes Eddie would finish them off, other times I would. They never seemed to catch on and Eddie always bought the cokes.

We returned to the Travis often, Eddie conducting business, me learning the trade. Eventually I was picking up betting cards for Eddie, travelling with him on the subway to the far corners of town I had never seen before. Harvard Square, where Eddie ran a sports book that actually took action on Wimbledon tennis and the pro golf tour, the North End with its back room poker parlors, Southie for the pool tables, Chinatown for pai gow and mah johng, everywhere for the sheer excitement.

Eddie and I double dated a lot, me with Susan, Eddie with a firecracker of a girl named Terasina Angelina Maria Guadalupe Gonzales. Tina for short. Tina was a dancer, a rock & roller supreme and Eddie had the best moves I'd seen since Teddy took the floor with Linda Rogers all those years ago. Doo wop was their backbeat and together they slipped, slid and strolled to the Penguins, Del Vikings, Marcels, Jive Five and their Elvis, Dion "The Wanderer" DiMucci. I tried a stroll or two with Susan but had no more success than I did with The Twist, back in the day.

Making the rounds with Eddie we ate pizza at Regina's, knocks and beans at Durgin Park and clam chowder at the Union Oyster House. I was becoming a bit of a man about town. I was picking up an education all right, but not much of it was taking place at Suffolk University. The implications of which I found out when mid-term grades were announced.

In between my travels with Eddie I was still making classes. I had dug deeper into the works of Kurt Vonnegut, discovered John Steinbeck, Virginia Wolfe and William Faulkner, learned that World War I and World War II were basically the same war with a twenty year recess, and digested a lot of buzz words from Psychology and Sociology 101. But I hadn't actually learned much except what I was learning on the street.

Then the hammer fell.

"Wow, you need a 2.0 to keep your student deferment, Dave. 1.8 ain't gonna' cut it," Eddie chastened me over coffee.

"Yeah, I've already got a notice of reclassification from the draft board. Suffolk's putting me on academic probation." This was news I hadn't broken to my parents yet. Not to anybody actually, besides Eddie.

"You can turn that around no sweat," Eddie offered. "You didn't get those grades for being stupid, you got them for being dumb."

"Thanks Eddie, that's just what I needed to hear." Indifferent as I had become to college the specter of the draft was real and, for guys in my position, imminent.

"You gotta' keep your seat on the gravy train," Eddie said, "Do the work, fly the flag, show the colors. You aren't failin' from lack of brains, you're failing from lack of effort."

Which was true. I had about six months to get back on "the gravy train," raise my academic average and regain my immunity form the draft. It was time to realign my priorities, change my focus and make up my mind what I was going to do with the rest of my life and how I was going to do it.

I wasn't going to get that chance. And neither was Eddie.

*Up in the morning and out to school,*
*The teacher is teaching the Golden Rule,*

*American History and Practical Math,*
*You studyin' hard and hopin' to pass,*

*Workin' your fingers right down to the bone,*
*And the guy behind you won't leave you alone.*

*Ring, ring goes the bell,*
*The cook in the lunch room's ready to sell,*

*Your lucky if you can find a seat,*
*You're fortunate if you have time to eat,*

*Back in the classroom, open your books,*
*Gee but the teacher don't know how mean she looks.*

*Hail, Hail Rock & Roll,*
*Deliver me from the days of old,*

*Long live Rock & Roll,*
*The beat of the drums loud and bold,*

*Rock, Rock, Rock & Roll,*
*The feelin' is there body and soul.*

Even if we weren't going to be.

"School Day", Written and recorded by Chuck Berry in 1957. Reached # 3 on the Billboard charts. Chuck Berry's multiple top ten hits also include "Johnny B. Goode", "Maybellene", "Sweet Little 16" "Rock & Roll Music" and "My Ding-A-Ling", his only #1 Billboard chart record.

# Chapter Eighteen

## *Letter From Teddy*

When the letter from Teddy finally arrived he had been gone over five months. Teddy signed up for the Marine Corps right after New Year's, 1966. Sergeant Woods had arranged it so that he would depart for Parris Island Boot Camp training the first week of February, and he did. At first Teddy was excited to go but as the day got closer I could see that he was maybe having second thoughts. His father and sister were quite upset when he told them his plans, especially since Chris was recovering from his wounds. Teddy decided not to tell Chris because he was afraid Chris would be mad at him too.

As I watched him walk away that day at the train station I thought of Margaret Mary waving goodbye at the airport after Christmas and how much emptier Lowell had seemed without her. Now Teddy would be gone too. No, there was just me, doing what I wasn't sure I wanted to be doing, going nowhere at all.

By this time the war in Vietnam was more and more in the news. Nightly newscasts showed helicopters full of soldiers landing in rice fields. Smoking tree lines and burning villages were two or three minute segments of the regular news parade. Local sports and weather was fifteen minutes. Margaret Mary and Peter Rayburn, when they were home for Christmas, were on fire about the war. Both were unsure as yet as to the righteousness or morality of the war but they were adamant that the burden of loss suffered in this conflict would be borne by our generation.

"Do you remember what President Johnson said when he was trying to get elected? About not sending American boys off to fight an Asian war?" Peter demanded, "All he's done since he's been in office is send American soldiers to fight in Vietnam."

"He more than doubled the number of soldiers fighting there! It's unbelievable!" Margaret Mary reminded. "And there is no indication that things are getting any better over there, only worse." Her voice rang with passion as she spoke with Peter and I, who were potentially cannon fodder, one small draft classification removed.

I kept hearing Teddy's long ago voice in my ear as he spoke about Lyndon Baines Johnson. "That guy looks like a crook to me," Teddy would say and we did not, at the time, listen.

Margaret Mary and Peter did not know at the time of this discussion, of Teddy's decision to enlist, or of my growing dissatisfaction with school and temptation to follow Teddy into the military. On this I kept my own counsel as the war clouds over our country darkened and, one small event at a time, the war machine was getting up to speed.

Only this January the Pentagon announced that American troop strength in Vietnam had topped two hundred thousand men. The First Marine Division had landed over four thousand fresh Marines at Chu Lai and the Army's 25th Infantry landed a similar number of ground combat troops at a place called Vung Tau.

Operation Rolling Thunder, the B-52 bomber strike raids on North Vietnam, intensified with fifty-eight separate bombing missions on January 31st alone. And quietly, in a separate barely noticed press release, American casualties in Vietnam for 1965 were announced as one thousand nine hundred and twenty-eight Killed In Action, approximately 160 per month, 40 per week, six a day, every day. And the beat went on.

Meanwhile the Beatles! were telling us "We Can Work It Out" and Simon & Garfunkel introduced us to "The Sound of Silence" while the Beach Boys sang cheerfully about "Ba-Ba-Ba, Ba- Barbara Ann." Top 40 radio relentlessly ran through our heads day in and out promising us "True Love", "Good Times", "Good Vibrations", and "California Dreamin'". It was perfect as long as you were something else besides Draft status I-A.

Amidst this clatter a former Green Beret Sergeant named Barry Sadler who had been wounded in Vietnam released a song he wrote while in the hospital recuperating from his injuries. "The Ballad of the Green Berets" rose to Number 1 on the Billboard charts and stayed there for five weeks. The lyrics of the song went like this,

*Fighting soldiers from the sky,*

*Fearless men who jump and die,*

*Men who mean just what they say,*

*The brave men of the Green Beret.*

*Silver wings upon their chest,*

*These are men, America's best,*

*One hundred men will test today,*

*But only three win the Green Beret.*

And so on.

The song's enormous popularity reflected the mind-set of a large part of society. Duty, Honor, Country were still values to be esteemed, passed on to a new generation. We were the new generation and the passing was not going smoothly. A sort of generational schizophrenia was setting in.

Anti-war movements continued to flourish. Organizations such as the "Students for a Democratic Society (SDS)" prospered on college campuses and were noisily opposed to the war in Vietnam. A civil rights movement which dubbed itself the "Student Non Violent Coordinating Committee (SNCC)" became the first primarily Black organization to publicly oppose the war in Vietnam. In their widely published manifesto they declared…

"We are in sympathy with, and support, the men in this country who are unwilling to respond to a military draft which would compel them to contribute their lives to the United States aggression in Viet Nam in the name of the freedom we find so false in this country."

SNCC and the SDS found immediate support among the so-called intelligentsia, on the college campuses and in celebrity circles. Most notable of these was Corretta Scott

King, wife of Martin Luther King, who also became a vocal opponent of the war, Joan Baez, folk singer and pacifist who lent her voice and support to a number of high profile protests along with Bob Dylan, Tom Paxton, and Phil Ochs, who saw his protest song, "I Ain't Marchin' Anymore" gain major airplay across the country. His lyrics went like this…

It's always the old who lead us to the wars,
Always the young to fall.

Now look at all we have won,
With the sword and the gun.

Tell me is it worth it all?
I Ain't Marchin' Anymore.

Meanwhile I marched, head down, to the commuter train every morning for my ride to Boston and to Suffolk University. I sat in classes, got the gist, repeated it back and prospered. Time went on, weeks went by, and finally my Freshman year ended. With a great sense of "So What" I returned to Lowell for the summer. And still hadn't heard a word from Teddy.

After Teddy had been gone about a month I went next door and asked Connie if they had heard anything. She told me they had received one package, Teddy's civilian clothes, mailed home from boot camp and a short note saying he was alright and would write when he had the chance. More weeks went by, then a month and no word. Finally, during the first week of my summer hiatus from school I went to see Sergeant Woods and told him how worried I was about Teddy.

"Parris Island can get pretty intense, Dave," Sergeant Woods explained. "Mostly what recruits do is eat, sleep and train, round the clock, seven days a week. I'll call a buddy of mine down there and have him check it out. If we make an official request and Teddy gets called into his Commanding Officer's office he could get in trouble. I'll check today and call you as soon as I know."

And he did. Sergeant Woods was a good guy. He said his buddy found out Teddy's cycle is out on bivouac, camping in the woods for the next week. He talked to Teddy's Drill Instructor who said Teddy is doing well, but they are pushing this cycle pretty hard. The DI said he would encourage Teddy to write home when they got back from the field.

Shortly afterward Connie told me they got a letter from Teddy saying he was fine and was sorry he did not have a chance to write before. Connie showed me the letter, it went like this,

Dear Dad and Connie,

I'm sorry I haven't had a chance to write before. We are training night and day and I am either too tired or too busy to write at the end of the day. I am very proud to say I am becoming a Marine, just like Chris. Even though we work very hard they are pretty good to us here. I remember what Sergeant Woods told me before I went in, to remember they are doing this for me, not to me. Marines don't get to be the best fighters in the world by doing the easy thing so neither will I.

I miss you both and will try to write more often. Say hi to Dave for me and tell him he'll get a letter real soon. I have to stop now because they are putting the lights out and I am going on guard duty. If you hear from Chris tell him hello for me,

Your proud Marine son and brother,

Ted

It was several more weeks before my letter finally came. It read,

Hi Dave,

Tomorrow I leave Parris Island for good. I'm sorry I haven't written before but the training here is hard and there has not been a lot of time for anything except training and eating and sleeping. The package of letters and stamps you gave me got all wet and I had to throw them away. We get up every morning at 4:30 and train till after dark. There's lots of push ups and long runs with all your gear and getting screamed at. But when you are done you are the roughest and toughest you can be. If you think we worked hard to get in shape at the gym, think again. I was in pretty good shape when I got here, (except for the smoking). I gave that up right away. I haven't had a cigarette in like six months and I don't want one.

I can honestly say that the Marine Corps is the hardest thing I have ever done. Even when Chris told me how brutal it was I really didn't think it was going to be this bad. Oh, and you know how you don't like getting needles? Well you get LOTS of them in the Marine Corps. I got shots for things I never even heard of and some of them hurt, a lot. Just so you know, alright?

When I finished boot camp I thought the hardest part of my training was over. Boy, was I wrong. Advanced Individual Training, also called Marine Combat Training is where the real hard stuff begins I am trained as an assistant automatic rifleman. I think this is the same thing Chris did. I hope so. I got one letter from him and he was pretty mad that I had joined up without telling him. I haven't written back to him yet but I'm sure he knows how busy we are and will understand. He's back in San Diego now and he's a Sergeant! I hope I can do that good if I get sent to Vietnam which is what is probably going to happen.

Our drill sergeants never stop telling us that we have to be ready to go into combat and that if we don't pay attention we will get killed or get another Marine killed. There's lots of talk about killing, Dave. Really killing. We practice stabbing people with bayonets and yelling Kill! As loud as we can. They show us how to choke a guy to death and where to hit him with your rifle to kill him. I'm not sure I could really do that. I've never told this to anybody before but I don't know if I could really kill a guy. But that's what Marines are for, they tell us that every day. Every night when they play "Taps" over a loudspeaker I think of all the Marines who have already been killed and hope I won't be one of them. I didn't think about getting scared when I joined up but now I think about it all the time. Don't tell anybody, okay?

How is Margaret Mary doing in Chicago? Is Peter still in priest school? Do you ever hear from any of the guys down at the gym. Say hello to Max for me and tell him I'm still keeping my left hand up. I never gave much thought to how much I was going to miss all of you but I sure think about it a lot now.

There's one more thing and that is why I'm writing this letter.

Our drill instructors told us today that before any Marine can leave Parris Island he has to make out his last will. Then they made us sit down and write our own. I'm sending mine to you in case something happens to me.

Folded within Teddy's letter was a one sheet, hand written:

**"Last Will and Testament of Pvt. Theodorus Gianoulous, USMC 2031162."**

My hands were shaking when I unfolded it and read…

I want my Marine Corps Insurance to go to my sister Connie and my brother Chris. They can split it even. My Dad can sell my car and use the money for whatever he wants. If I have any pay or money on my pay book please use it to have a nice dinner on me. There's a box of stuff in my closet that I want my friend, Dave Ferrier to have. I wrote my name on it and it should be easy to find. I guess that's it.

And one more thing, if I get killed, I want to be buried in my Marine uniform with all the medals and awards and badges I rate on me.

Thank You,

**Pvt. T. Gianoulous**

As I read this I started to cry. I couldn't help it. It wasn't just the thought that Teddy could get killed, though this fact choked me as I read. I was crying for how much my whole life was changing, and how suddenly I was being overwhelmed by the changes. I could never have imagined that one day I would be reading my Best Buddy's Last Will and Testament, but I was. I took several deep breaths to pull myself together, then carefully refolded Teddy's Will and read the last part of his letter. It read…

Dave, there's something else I should tell you about joining the Marines and I hope I don't get in trouble for it. Maybe don't. It's not like what we thought. It's more about killing people, and being there when your friends get killed. I know you are a lot smarter than me and read a lot of books and stuff but I know things now that you don't. Some of them are not good and I wish I didn't know them. I am going to be the best Marine I can but I hope I never have to kill anybody and I hope you won't have to either.

I've got to go now, our sergeants are yelling for us to finish up and get our gear together. I'll write again when I can and I hope you will write to me too when I have an address.

Your friend,

Ted.

Looking back I think that was the beginning of the end for me. I was living in a shell. The country was changing, being torn in two by the Pro-War, Anti-War movement. Politicians seemed to be full of lies, their stories seemed to change every day. My friends had scattered, my purpose was unclear but from this point I realized I had to do something, whatever that something was.

Another crystal clear voice of our generation, my new-found poet and inspiration, Bob Dylan chimed in on what was happening among the younger generation. His "The times they are a-Changin'" concludes with the following lyric…

*The line it is drawn,*

*The curse it is cast,*

*The slow one now*

*Will later be fast,*

*And the present now*

*Will later be past,*

*The order is rapidly fadin',*

*And the first one now*

*Will later be last,*

*For the times they are a changin'.*

It was time for me to start changing with them.

Welcome to the
JEANNETTE RANKIN PEACE PARADE
END THE WAR IN VIETNAM AND SOCIAL CRISIS AT HOME !

# Chapter Nineteen

## *The Montreal Express*

As I had promised my Dad I was slogging through the fall semester at Suffolk University. I had chosen a slate of courses I hoped would re-ignite my fervor for education, and mend my academic probation status, with mixed results. A European history course revealed  that the leaders there were just as foolish and self-serving as ours were here. I don't know whether this was knowledge I needed at this point though.

I sat through a film history class, mostly silent films, black and white wonders which showed how far the industry had advanced and how much fun it had forgotten. My contemporary journalism course taught me the Who, What, Where, Why and How method of constructing a report. It was my favorite class and led me to write several articles for the school news sheet which weren't bad, pretty good actually. I tacked on a couple of bunny courses from the Sociology and Psychology department to insure I'd get my grade point average back up to student deferment status and there I was.

Susan and I were coupling frequently, once behind some bushes on the Boston Common at midnight. This was her idea, but I wish it had been mine. Susan was a pleasant companion and was going to make a terrific nurse, what she was not, or who she was not, was Margaret Mary, but more was to come on that later.

College was looking up, and then the worm turned.

"I gotta' leave town," Eddie announced one afternoon when we met for coffee at the Travis. Eddie sounded stressed, anxious and totally out of character. He was slouched in his chair, like he was trying to look small.

"Leave town why?" I asked, visions of bookie type gangsters closing in on my buddy. It was far worse than that.

"Actually," Eddie admitted, lowering his voice in the noisy room, "I'm leaving the country, going to Canada. My draft notice came. I ain't goin'."

This caught me completely by surprise. Eddie never struck me as the politically active type, unless he was taking bets on an election. I didn't know what to say. Eddie was staring at me waiting for a question. The silence thundered. Finally he spoke,

"Do you know who Tommy Marks is?"

I didn't.

"All city, all state halfback from Dorchester High two years ago. Him and me, we was best friends. Tommy even shot a better game of pool than me, coulda' turned pro. He had football scholarship offers from Notre Dame, Boston University, Northeastern, coupla' others. He joined the Marine Corps instead."

Eddie sat up straight, looked around the room. "If Tommy was here he's be the best lookin' most popular, happiest guy in the room, always smiling, he'd know everybody's name."

"I'm guessing Tommy isn't smiling any more." I tried sounding concerned, not pessimistic, though I had a pretty good guess at what Eddie was about to tell me.

"What Tommy ain't doin' is walkin' anymore. Got home from Nam coupla' weeks ago, lost both his legs to a land mine. When I heard he was home I went over to his house, talked to his Ma. She said Tommy was there but he didn't want to see anybody. Not even me."

Not killed then, I had already heard that Ron Bassett and Danny Higgins, two guys I went to Lowell high school with, had been killed in Vietnam. The Lowell Sun newspaper regularly ran very small obituaries of hometown guys who were being killed over there. Too regularly. It was only now occurring to me that death was not the only grim outcome from going there.

"I was gonna' leave, then I heard Tommy telling me to come on in." At this point, for the very first time, I saw Eddie's eyes fill with tears. His hands trembled as he reached for his coffee cup and he was choking on his words.

"Ever see what your best friend looked like if he didn't have any legs?" Eddie spit out the words, anger intermingled with pain, heartbreak demanding an answer. He was seeing Tommy. I was seeing Teddy.

For a moment, maybe more, we sat across from each other in stunned silence. I didn't know what to say, couldn't even begin to imagine I ever would.

"I ain't good about talkin' about this stuff, you know?" Eddie finally said in a half choked whisper. I wasn't very good at hearing about it either.

"Tommy looked like he weighed about ninety pounds, guy was 165 in high school. He was in this wheelchair and he had a blanket like across his legs, only there wasn't no legs under the blanket." That was it for Eddie, his voice choked up, his story ended. The silence roared back. We didn't look at one another.

"Hey Eddie, you got cards for this weekend's games?" A red headed kid with a very bad mustache was bouncing up and down on the balls of his feet standing next to the table. He had his hands jammed into his jacket pockets and kept looking around the room as if someone was chasing him.

"Not today, Lenny, tomorrow right here." Eddie's reply broke the gloom between us and Lenny slunk back into the crowd.

"Look, about that," Eddie was talking to me now, "I talked to some guys about you taking over my pad but they don't think you're the right guy for the job."

They were right, I wasn't. I didn't know whether to thank Eddie for trying to give me his sports pad or thank them for not giving it to me. But there were other matters to address.

"Eddie, have you thought this through? Going off to Canada, that's a pretty big step. You could go to jail if they catch you."

"Ain't gonna catch me. Canada don't send you back for evadin'. It's an asylum country."

I had heard of this movement of course. Both Canada and Sweden were accepting American draft resisters and even deserters and offering them political asylum. Draft evasion was not a criminal offense in Canada and desertion was not on the list of crimes for which a person could be extradited from Canada back to the United States.

A Toronto based anti-Draft Program published a book entitled "The Manual for Draft Age Immigrants to Canada" which sold over 100,000 copies.

"The hardest part is gonna' be leavin' my Ma," Eddie said. "She won't leave the apartment. Wants me to go though, she knows Tommy's mother real well. My Aunt Camille is gonna' come live with her though, stay in my room," Eddie hurried on with his explanation, seeking, I thought, some kind of permission.

"My Aunt Camille, she's my Ma's younger sister, never married. She's got a face would stop a Timex watch but a beautiful, beautiful heart. I'll be sendin' 'em a few bucks from Canada, help them get by."

"You sure about this, Eddie? Sure it's the right way to go?" I asked.

"Lookit'," Eddie began, jabbing his finger in my face for emphasis, "This ain't about me bein' scared, you know? This is about What for?" Eddie leaned across the table and spoke in an urgent whisper, "I ain't got no idea what we are fighting in Vietnam for, and I pay attention! The whole operation smells like a loser to me, and I know a loser when I see one."

Eddie was building up a head of steam, and I was starting to believe he was right.

"I ain't goin' to Canada because of politics. I'm goin' because I don't like bein' told what to do by people who can't explain why they're doin' it."

Eddie slowed down and continued in a softer, sadder voice, "You know what Tommy told me that day I saw him over at his house? He said, it ain't worth it. He said all his unit did was walk through the same jungle, the same villages, day after day, getting shot at, shooting people who may have been shooting at them and then doing the same thing, the next day and the day after that."

Eddie slammed back in his chair, finished, "If I got to choose between Vietnam and Canada, I'm takin' Canada, every time. Like Tommy shoulda'."

Eddie stood up to leave, extending his  hand to me for the farewell handshake. "One more thing before I go," he said looking around the coffee shop at the tables packed with earnest, eager students, "Lots of people around here are getting educated, don't ever confuse that with getting smart."

We shook hands and that was the last time I saw Eddie. I presumed he wasn't the stay in touch type but I wished him well and hoped he would remain safe, in Canada.

Losing Eddie, losing Teddy, losing Jimmy Barone, missing Margaret Mary, all these things were starting to add up for me and none of them would help me prepare for the next two blows. Two pieces of mail, one from strangers, one much worse, which were to come in the next two weeks. The weeks before Christmas. There wasn't going to be much Ho-Ho-Ho-ing this year.

The first piece of not so good news came in a brown envelope with a little window on the front that had my name and address along with my draft registration number. This couldn't be good. The letter arrived on December 8th, Teddy's birthday, and four days before my nineteenth.

Short and sweet it told me I must report to the Boston Naval Yard Annex for my Draft Physical on January 16th, five weeks from today. It seemed my efforts to mend my academic standing had been too little too late, perhaps.

I showed the letter to my Dad. He read it with a grave expression and asked, "What are you going to do son?"

Just to let me know I had a choice. I told him I was going. I couldn't bear to see an expression of disappointment on his face again. And other than following Eddie to Canada, what choice did I have?

There were a number of organizations scattered around the Boston campuses which offered draft counseling, or more accurately draft evasion counseling.

They offered the criteria for exhibiting a number of physical debilitations which would result in a medical deferment, such as ruptured spleens, flat feet, asthma, poor eyesight, even horrible hygiene. There was no way I could ever have gone that route.

There were mental health deferments, schizophrenia, paranoia, clinical depression and bat shit crazy. Also in this category one could be deferred by stating he was a homosexual. Nothing for me there either.

Some geniuses believed you would fail your draft physical if you ate a LOT of bananas before the exam. Others, believed in the disqualifying powers of sunflower seeds? Or maybe sesame seeds? Poppy seeds? Marijuana seeds would work as well. Not going there as well.

A final option was to just flat out refuse the draft. Show up, say no and accept the consequences. The consequences however were up to five years in Federal prison and a $25,000 fine. Not for me.

Getting your notice for a draft physical didn't necessarily mean you were definitely going into the Army. But it did mean they were seriously considering it.

"I'm going to go, Dad. If I get called I go in." I tried to make it sound like I was making a decision rather than letting the draft board make a decision for me.

That hung a bit of a pall over Christmas on Glenmere Street but nothing like the veil of gloom my next piece of mail would bring. A Christmas card. A Christmas card from Margaret Mary.

The envelope was Red, Christmassy red. It was thick, there was a letter in the card. The card was cute, the letter would break my heart.

Here is what the letter said,

Dearest David,

I am writing to let you know I am leaving school right after Christmas and moving to Colorado with Kendall. I am not quitting school. I am taking a leave of absence to be with Kendall on a commune near Denver, Colorado. I love him. We have been living together for the past four months and I have kept this from you because I know you are struggling with your schoolwork and I didn't want to upset you.

You are, and have always been, and always will be my dearest, best friend. I hope that never changes. Kendall says our friends are the family that we get to choose in life. I will always choose you.

I hope school is going well. Have you written any new stories? I'd love to read them. Kendall says you must be quite a writer if you made my top ten list. You will always be at the head of my top ten list.

Please do not be angry with me. I did not plan for things to go this way. I did fall in love with Kendall and I hope you will understand that. But the rest, leaving school, going to the commune, I never foresaw. So much has changed in the world. I fear this war in Vietnam is going to consume us all. I worry so much for Teddy and I know that you are thinking about following him into the service as well. Please don't. I couldn't bear it if something were to happen to you.

I have promised Sean, and I am promising you that I will come back and finish school. Though I am looking forward to the experience of living on the commune I realize it is not my future. Perhaps, when it is all said and done, you are.

I only know I miss you and think about you every day. Please take care of yourself and stay in school, stay safe, until we meet again,

Love,
MM

Kendall still sounds like an asshole.

The rest of the year played out in grays and deep blues. There was a Christmas tree, gifts, a turkey and a sense of foreboding in our home.

Bob Hope went to Vietnam and gave 22 shows and visited five hospitals. He brought blond bombshell movie star Carroll Baker with him along with his steadfast troupe of Jerry Colonna, Kaye Stevens and the gorgeous Joey Heatherton. I was starting to wish I was there with him.

There was only one Christmas song that stuck in my head that year. Elvis Presley sang it and it went like this…

I'll have a Blue Christmas without you,
I'll be so blue, thinking about you,
Decorations of red on a
green Christmas tree,
Won't be the same dear If you're
not here with me.

And when those blue snow
flakes start falling,
That's when those blue memories
start calling,

You'll be doing alright with your
Christmas of White,

But I'll have a blue, blue Christmas.

And I did.

# Chapter Twenty

## Hail & Farewell

I see a red door and I want it painted black,
No colors anymore I want them to turn black,

I see the girls go by dressed in
their summer clothes
I have to turn my head until the darkness goes.

I see a line of cars and they're all painted black
With flowers and my love,
Both never to come back.

I've seen people turn their heads and
quickly look away,
Like a newborn baby it just happens everyday.

Maybe then I'll fade away and not have
to face the facts,
It's not easy facing up when your whole
world is black.

No more will my green sea go turn
a deeper blue,
I could not foresee this thing
happening to you.

If I look hard enough into the setting sun,
My love will laugh with me before
the morning comes.

I want to see it painted, painted BLACK.

BLACK as night, BLACK as coal,
I wanna' see the sun blotted out from the sky.

I wanna' see It painted, painted, painted
BLACK!

"Paint It Black", Written by Keith Richards and Mick Jagger. Recorded by the Rolling Stones and reaching #1 on the Billboard Charts in 1966. In 2018 the Ford Motor Company purchased the rights to this song for a car commercial.

That was me. In a nutshell. The lowest I have ever felt, the lowest I hope I ever feel. Welcome to January, February, 1967. It was not going to be my best year.

I had given up Edgar Allen Poe as too cheerful. I craved darkness, the dungeon, wherever I could find one. "I am a Rock" indeed. Nothing was working.

I had raised my grade point average at Suffolk to a healthy 3.2 (out of 4), a solid "B", but apparently it was too little, too late. When I reported to the Naval Yard for my draft physical on January 16th, I passed with flying colors and they told me I could expect a sixty to ninety day call up, March at the latest. School was out. There was no sense in re-enrolling for second semester if I was going to be drafted in March. I let the school know about this development. They treated me like I had a disease and wished me well.

There was total silence from Margaret Mary. Apparently Kendall was filling her calendar. I had not heard from Teddy since I received his Last Will and Testament. Eddie was in Canada, Jimmy Barone was in New York City. Susan was becoming geographically undesirable. Nelson's Gym was half empty, most of the guys I trained with had left town, joined the service or stopped training. Lowell felt, gray, lifeless, useless. Like me.

One afternoon I dropped by Sergeant Woods' office down at the Post Office in Lowell. He was no longer assigned there. I was told this by another crisply uniformed, refrigerator sized Staff Sergeant. He smiled at me like a wolf sizing up a sheep, came on a little too strong, and I backed out of the office.

Two doors down was the Army recruiter. I peeked in the door and met Master Sergeant Dontell Lewis. He looked up from behind his desk and smiled,

"Something I can do for you, son?"

The fatherly type. I already had one.

"Come on in son, I'm not going to bite you." Wolves in every office. I wasn't buying, but I walked in anyway.

I was more than a little impressed by the formidable number of stripes on the sleeves of Sergeant Lewis' uniform. Also he had a chest full of ribbons, a set of what I recognized as parachutist wings and a bright blue and silver Combat Infantryman's Badge. Impressive.

"Have a seat, son. Are you interested in joining the service?" The question sounded more cordial than carnivorous. I sat down and in short order I told him about my draft status, my educational background and my overwhelming sense of uncertainty about my future.

Sergeant Lewis didn't press. His next statement really impressed me though.

"Joining the service is not an answer to your problems, Dave. Do you mind if I call you Dave? The service is an opportunity, not a solution."

"An opportunity for what? Aren't most guys ending up in Vietnam getting their asses shot off?" I was trying to disguise despair with sarcasm.

"No, they are not," he answered calmly, "A considerable number of soldiers will be assigned to Vietnam. They are not there to "get their asses shot off," they are there to help the people of South Vietnam save their country from Communist aggression."

Another true believer, like Sergeant Woods. I liked Sergeant Woods.

"I'm sorry," I said, "I'm having a bad…month."

Sergeant Lewis laughed. He had a great laugh. He leaned into it and his face lit up like a candle. "This is definitely not the right place to come to fix a bad month."

I found myself relaxing a little, at least in the sense that I didn't feel as angry or as about to burst into tears as I had for the past few weeks.

"Look, Dave, lots of guys walk through my door looking for a solution to all their problems by joining the Army. What they are really trying to do is run away from their problems, and that, generally speaking, doesn't work."

"Do you have any idea what does work? I'm open to suggestions?"

Sergeant Lewis leaned back in his chair, giving me a long hard looking over. I felt uncomfortable under his stare but lately I had been feeling uncomfortable everywhere.

"Dave, I have been in the Army twenty-seven years, enlisted when I was 17 out of Dothan, Alabama. When I joined I could barely read or write. Sixth grade education, eleven brothers and sisters, I was the oldest."

"Wow," I thought, this was miles from Glenmere Street and all my troubles. Sergeant Lewis wasn't complaining, he was explaining. I was listening.

"I now have a Master's Degree in Business Administration I earned while I was stationed out at Fort Lewis, Washington. I've been to Europe, Asia, Africa and Australia and just about every state in the United States. I fought in Korea and Vietnam. I am married and have three children, two in college, one a registered nurse. None of this would have been possible if I had stayed in Dothan, Alabama."

"So the Army was a solution for you." I replied, clinging to the wrong answer.

"No, it was not. The Army was an opportunity, like I said. I made the most of that opportunity and it became a solution, but I worked hard at it. The one thing I can tell you for absolute sure about the Army is that you will get out of it every bit as much as you put into it."

True believer. I needed to hear from somebody who was a true believer about anything positive or negative. There were a lot of both kinds around lately.

Sergeant Lewis continued, "The hard fact Dave, is that you are going to be drafted in about six weeks. You either report or you don't. Whatever decision you make, that decision is going to stay with you for the rest of your life. You need to think hard on it, really hard. Then come back and see me before you make up your mind. Deal?"

He reached across his desk and held out his hand. I shook it and replied, "Deal."

No hustle, no pressure, no bullshit. Not what I was expecting. I left the office feeling less pessimistic, less cynical and really needing to have a long talk with my Dad.

We went to Lefty's on a mutual agreement to cut back on our donut consumption. It was Saturday morning, it was snowing pretty hard. The plows were out clearing the streets and the forecast called for another foot of snow before the end of the day.

Dad and I settled into a back corner table, coffees in our hands. The restaurant was empty. A couple of feet of falling snow will do that.

"I talked to an Army recruiter yesterday, Dad," I began.

"Did you sign anything?" He wanted to know.

"He never asked me to. He didn't even try to get me to sign up. He just said I should think carefully about what I wanted to do and then come back and see him."

"Sounds like a good man. What's his name?"

"Sergeant Woods. He's a Master Sergeant, chest full of medals and ribbons. I really liked him."

"That's probably why they made him a recruiter son. Liking him doesn't mean you're going to like the Army."

"Did you like the Army, Dad?" I wasn't changing the subject. I really wanted to know.

"I did. The Army gave me a chance to grow up away from home and away from everything being at home limited me to."

That took a minute to process. Somewhere in my head a very dim light bulb came on. Not on enough though.

"What do you mean, Dad? I don't understand."

My Dad sipped his coffee, gathered his thoughts and replied,

"David, up till now you've done about everything we've ever asked of you. You've done well in school, kept out of trouble and been a good son. Your mother and I are proud of you."

That felt good, a lot better than anything else had been feeling lately.

"But up till now everything you've done has been pretty much what we expected you to do and you've done it mainly because you knew we expected it, right?"

Right. And Wrong.

"Your mother and I want you to do the right thing about being drafted. We don't want to see you sent to Vietnam and be injured or killed, but we do want you to do what you think is right here. Either you go, or you choose not to. Make it your choice, not our expectation. Whatever you decide will be alright with us."

As we spoke, in the accumulating snowfall the country was being torn in two by the Vietnam War. Not even quite a war yet, still a "conflict' which didn't make a bit of difference to the guys being killed over there. Or to Tommy Marks.

On the college campuses the anti-war movement flourished, sure they were right by staying far to the left. In the shipyards and factories hard hats with red, white and blue flag decals shouted "Your Country, Right or Wrong" without fully considering the "wrong" possibility.

So here I sat, receiving encouragement and permission from my Dad which helped, of course. I still didn't know what to do, but I realized I had to make up my own mind about what I was going to do. I thought of Jimmy Barone, exiled to New York with his "pansy artist" brother. I wondered how Eddie was doing in Montreal. Best guess is he was learning a lot about betting on professional hockey. Teddy's words, or word, "Don't" came to mind as well. I would have loved to talk this over, and over, with Margaret Mary of course, but there was the whole Kendall thing. Peter Rayburn was in Newburgh, New York in a seminary and I was here, with my Dad, making the biggest decision of my life as the snow piled up outside the windows.

"So what are the benefits of enlisting instead of just waiting to be drafted?"

I was back in Sergeant Lewis' office with questions, still no answers.

Sergeant Lewis folded his hands on his desk and answered evenly, "The first thing you should consider, Dave, is that enlisting is a three year commitment. Drafted is two."

I let that sink in. The Navy, Air Force and Marines were four year commitments. I needed more information.

"If you are drafted you will be assigned a job, we call this a Military Occupational Specialty, an "MOS", by the military. These jobs are assigned by the immediate needs of the service."

Sergeant Lewis looked me straight in the eye, his voice grim.

"These days the needs of the service are mainly trigger pullers, combat infantryman. MOS - 11B20. The more cynical out there refer to them as bullet stoppers."

I swallowed, hard.

He continued, "I was an Eleven Bravo Twenty. It is by far, the hardest, most fundamental and essential job in the military. The only skill you need to be a combat infantryman is to learn to control your fear. Some call that courage. I consider it an honor to have been one."

"But you are not one now?" I added.

"I am not. Between Korea and Vietnam I decided I wanted to better myself, to get some training that did not require shooting a gun. I took some correspondence courses, got my high school diploma and Bachelor's degree. Even finished my Masters out in Washington before I came here. The Army paid for it all. Like I said, opportunities, not solutions."

"What opportunities would I get if I signed up?" I wanted to know.

"Depends," he answered honestly. "What opportunities did you have in mind?"

"My Dad was a tail gunner on B-24 bombers," I answered, without really knowing why.

"Army doesn't have tail gunners anymore," he chuckled, "B-24's either. What about aviation, helicopters maybe?"

Helicopters. First time I'd ever thought of that.

"The Air Force handles most of the fixed wing flying for the military these days. All the bombers, and they do not have tail gunners. You seem like you have a good head on your shoulders, got some college. You could probably qualify for Warrant Officer school, become a helicopter pilot. The Army's needing a lot of helicopter pilots these days."

Now that was something I had never even considered. Helicopter pilot sounded interesting.

"You mean the Army would teach me to fly?"

"If you qualify for the training they will. One catch though, it's a four year commitment. They teach you to fly they want an extra year."

That sounded fair, sort of. But four years was a long time.

"What type of qualifications would I have to have?" I was nibbling at the bait. Sergeant Lewis was kind enough not to set the hook.

'You have what? A year and half of college?" He asked.

"Three semesters. I passed all my courses."

"Yet here you are." As he let me back down to earth. "That's good. There are some written tests on which I'm sure you will do fine, a background check and that's about it. Do you know what a Warrant Officer is?"

I had no idea.

"In your case, he's basically a pilot. He gets all the benefits an officer gets and he gets flight pay," Sergeant Lewis explained.

"Anything else?" I asked.

"Well, in my experience, Warrant Officers are excellent pilots. Flyboys, we call them. Ten feet from an aircraft they are tits on a bull so to speak, but don't ever tell anyone I said so."

Flyboys sounded great. Tits on a bull I already felt like.

"I'd like to talk this over with my parents one more time Sergeant Lewis. Would that be okay?"

"Exactly what I would recommend. Come let me know when you have made up your mind."

We shook hands once again. I left his office feeling close to my decision and grateful that I was not being pressured or prodded into making it. Now there was just the talk with my parents.

This took place around our kitchen table. My Mother, Father and both brothers were there.

"I've decided to enlist in the Army," I began. Mom's eyes got a little wider, my Dad sat up straight, my brothers broke out in big smiles. "I talked to a recruiter downtown and he's going to get me into helicopter training."

This last part came as a surprise to everybody, just as it had to me two days earlier.

"Cool!" My brother John said. Not so cool my Mother's expression said.

"The recruiter said he can get you into pilot school?" My Dad asked.

"He said I was qualified. There are some written tests and stuff but I believe Sergeant Lewis, he's a real good guy."

"I'd like to meet him sometime," My Father said.

"Maybe on Saturday," I answered. "I called him today and he said he'd be there."

And that was pretty much it. We talked more, about how long I would be gone, where I would be going, how I should keep safe, but the deal was done. My mind was made up and after Saturday I would be off to helicopter pilot school.

Man plans, God laughs.

Onward.

"A song is a song. But there are some songs, ah, some songs are the greatest. The Beatles sang "Yesterday". Listen to the lyrics."

**-Chuck Berry**

# YESTERDAY

Yesterday, All my troubles seemed so far away,
Now it looks as though they're here to stay,
Oh, I believe in yesterday.

Suddenly, I'm not half the man I used to be,
There's a shadow hanging over me,
Oh, yesterday came suddenly.

Why she had to go? I don't know,
She wouldn't say,
I said something wrong,
Now I long for yesterday.

Yesterday, Love was such an easy game to play,
Now I need a place to hide away,
Oh, I believe in yesterday.

**_If you enjoyed this book, please take a few moments to write a review on your favorite store, and refer it to your friends. Share your views, how else will anyone know?_**

Read the first book in this Series, *"Born On A Mountaintop"* to find out the back story of David and his friends earlier years leading up to Raised on A Rock.

Available on Amazon, Barnes & Noble and other stores
(Paperback, eBook formats).

# Song Glossary

Some are silly, some are sad, some are joyous, some are mad, all are precious in their time and place. In order they are:

"Do You Want To Know A Secret", Lennon/McCartney (mostly Lennon), released March 3, 1963. The first Beatles top ten single, #2 on Billboard Charts to feature George Harrison as lead singer.

"No Particular Place To Go", Chuck Berry, released May 1964. Reached #10 on Billboard charts. Berry was a master of the "car" song, a master of "R&R Music". John Lennon was quoted as saying, "If you had to give Rock&Roll another name, you might call it Chuck Berry."

"I'd Be A Legend In My Time", Don Gibson, released 1960. Originally a "B" side of "Far, Far, Away", didn't chart. Covered in 1974 by Ronnie Milsap, went to #1 on the country charts.

"My Girl", written by Smokey Robinson, recorded by the Temptations. Released December, 1964. Reached #1 on the Billboard Charts.

"Let It Snow!", Written by Sammy Kahn and Julie Styne. First performed by Vaughn Monroe (with the Norton Sisters) in 1945. A perennial which reached #1 for five weeks upon release.

"What A Wonderful World It Would Be", Written by Sam Cooke, Herb Alpert and Lou Adler. Recorded by Sam

Cooke, Released in April, 1964. Reached #12 on the Billboard charts.  Re-released in 1978 after being featured in the film, "Animal House" and reached # 2 on the charts.

"Eve of Destruction", Written by P.F. Sloan, recorded by Barry McGuire.  Released in August, 1965. Reached #1 on Billboard charts despite being banned from all radio play in Scotland.

"Blowin' In The Wind", Written and recorded by Bob Dylan, released 1963. Covered by Peter, Paul & Mary that same year and reached  #2 on Billboard Charts. "Blowin' In The Wind" was ranked #14 on Rolling Stones poll of the "500 Greatest Songs Of All Time".

"Where Have All The Flowers Gone?, Written by Pete Seeger and Joe Hickerson in 1961. A Kingston Trio cover rose to #21 on the Billboard Charts.

"Yesterday", Written by Lennon/McCartney (All McCartney). Reached #1 on the Billboard charts in July, 1965. "Yesterday" was the first solo performance released by the Beatles. The song was voted, "Best Song of the 20th Century" 1n a 1969 BBC Radio Poll and the #1 Pop Song of all time by both MTV and Rolling Stone magazine.

"Please Mr. Postman", Written by William Garrett and Marvin Gaye. Recorded by The Marvelettes.  Reached #1 on the Billboard Charts in 1961. "Mr. Postman" was the first #1 hit for Motown Records.

"Help", Written by Lennon/McCartney (Mostly Lennon). Reached #1 on the Billboard charts in 1965. "Help!" was used as the title for the second Beatles movie. It was also the first Beatles tune used in a commercial when, in 1985 the Ford Motor Company paid $100,000 for the tune to sell cars?

"I Can't Get No Satisfaction", which when read literally means "I Can Get Satisfaction" was written by Keith Richards and Mick Jagger of the Rolling Stones. It reached #1 on the Billboard charts in June of 1965. In February of 1966 the Rolling Stones performed this song on the Ed Sullivan show only to have the lyric "Trying to get some girl" bleeped out by the censors. Times, they were a changin'.

"Save The Last Dance For Me", Written by Doc Pomus and Mort Shuman, recorded by The Drifters eventually reached #1 on the Billboard charts despite being released as a "B" side to "Nobody But Me" on Atlantic Reords. Dick Clark flipped the record over on American Bandstand and a classic was discovered.

"I'm So Lonesome I Could Cry", Written and recorded by Hank Williams in 1949. Covered by B. J. Thomas in 1966 it reached #8 on the billboard charts for that year. This song was rated #111 on Rolling Stones poll of "The Greatest Hits of All Time, the only song from the 1940's to be ranked.

"Nowhere To Run", Written by Brian Holland, Lamont Dozier and Eddie Holland. Recorded by Martha & The Vandellas in 1965 when it rose to #8 on the Billboard charts.

"Travelin' Man", Written by Jerry Fuller, recorded by Ricky Nelson. Reached #1 on the Billboard charts in 1961. Recorded with the Jordanaires, Elvis Presley's back up vocalists, it was Nelson's last top ten hit until "Garden Party" reached #6 in 1972.
"Jingle Bell Rock", Written by Joe Beale and Jim Boothe, recorded by Bobby Helms in 1957. Reached #3 on Billboard charts. The flip side of this perennial is the

immortal, "Captain Santa Claus and His Reindeer Spacemen." Go figure.

<u>"The Christmas Song"</u>, Written by Mel Torme and Bob Wells, Recorded by Nat King Cole in 1946. It has been re-released every year since.

<u>"I'm Happy Just To Dance With You"</u>, Written by Lennon/McCartney. Lead vocal by George Harrison. Reached #95 on Billboard charts in 1964. Recorded in four takes.

<u>"Will You Love Me Tomorrow?"</u>, Written by Carole King and Gerry Goffin. Recorded by The Shirelles. It reached #1 on the Billboard charts in 1960, the first #1 hit by a black female singing group.

<u>"School Is Out"</u>, Written by Gary U.S. Bonds and Gene Barge, recorded by Gary U.S. Bonds in 1961. Song is from Bond's only million selling album, "Dance To Quarter To Three". In 1963 Bonds toured England headlining above The Beatles.

<u>"Sounds of Silence"</u>, Written by Paul Simon, recorded by Simon and Garfunkel. Reached #1 on the Billboard charts on January 1, 1966, months after Paul Simon and Art Garfunkel mutually decided to stop recording together.

<u>"The Times They Are A-Changing"</u>, Written and recorded by Bob Dylan on his album of the same name. Re-recorded and released by The Byrds in 1965. "Times" was voted #54 on Rolling Stones poll of "The Greatest Hits of All Time."
<u>"Say Hey Willie"</u>, Written by Willard Robinson, recorded by The Treniers in 1954. This baseball gem was produced by a twenty-one year old novice named Quincy Jones.

"School Day", Written and recorded by Chuck Berry in 1957. Reached #3 on the Billboard charts. Chuck Berry's multiple top ten hits also include "Johnny B. Goode", "Maybellene", "Sweet Little 16" "Rock & Roll Music" and "My Ding-A-Ling", his only #1 Billboard chart record.

"Ballad of the Green Berets", Written and recorded by Staff Sergeant Barry Sadler while in an Army hospital recovering from wounds he received in Vietnam. Held #1 on the Billboard charts for five weeks and was the biggest selling single of 1966.

"I Ain't Marchin' Anymore", Written and recorded by Phil Ochs in 1965. Ochs described himself as a "singing journalist" and was extremely active in the anti-war movement in the mid to late sixties. Ochs committed suicide in 1976. He was 35 years old.

"Blue Christmas", Written by Billy Hayes and Jay Johnson and first recorded by Doyle Odell in 1948. The song became immortalized when Elvis Presley included it on his first Christmas album released in 1957.

"Paint It Black", Written by Keith Richards and Mick Jagger. Recorded by the Rolling Stones and reaching #1 on the Billboard Charts in 1966.

"Universal Soldier", Written and recorded by Buffy St. Marie in 1963. Re-released and covered by folk singer Donavan in 1965 when it reached # 53 on the Billboard charts.